THE HAUNTINGS OF LIVINGSTONE HALL

AN ANTHOLOGY OF GHOSTLY STORIES

EBONY MCKENNA   SARAH J WOLFE

ALISON STUART   ELIZA RENTON   CAROL CHALLIS

DENISE OGILVIE   LOUISE REYNOLDS

Edited by

EBONY MCKENNA

OPORTET PUBLISHING

Copyright © 2017 by the Saturday Ladies' Bridge Club

Carol Challis, Ebony McKenna, Denise Ogilvie, Eliza Renton, Louise Reynolds, Alison Stuart, Sarah J Wolfe

Published by Oportet Publishing, 2017

Print ISBN 978-0-9954341-3-4

CONTENTS

LIVINGSTONE HALL HOTEL AND SPA

*H*istory … history … history!

The very stones of this Grade II listed building, snuggled in the folds of the Gloucestershire countryside, exude history. The home of the Compton-Barr family for centuries, the current building is Jacobean but built on the site of much earlier buildings, dating back to Roman times or earlier.

LIVINGSTONE HALL HOTEL and SPA is the perfect venue for that special event or that weekend getaway from the stress of life in the big city! Staying at Livingstone Hall transports you back to a more gracious time.

The beautifully maintained house boasts 25 bedrooms, a large dining hall, ballroom and various 'break-out' rooms. Outside you can enjoy lawn tennis courts, the lake, a roof-top golf tee, and an indoor swimming pool and spa, available throughout the year.

With its huge ballroom and large panelled hall, we can seat up to 150 at a banquet or wedding and an onsite event planner is available to make sure your special event goes without a hitch. Or if you prefer the *'plein air'*, our romantic Grecian Temple is the perfect spot to make your vows.

Other on-site activities include swimming, golf, bumper balls, fishing, pedalos, tennis, horseriding, croquet and archery. Never a dull moment!

And there is absolutely NO truth to the stories about Livingstone Hall being the most haunted house in Gloucestershire! The locals will have their fun . . .

I'M RIGHT HERE : EBONY MCKENNA

*P*aradise Compton-Barr winced with embarrassment as the ceremony began. Her mother, Summer Tourmaline, lit the final candle and took her seat at the head of the table. 'Let's join hands and call upon those spirits present to make themselves known.'

Reaching her bejewelled fingers to those either side of her, Summer took her friends' hands in hers. Collectively, their silver-streaked hair tangled in their beads and hooped earrings as they swayed their heads and hummed, trying to catch each other's tunes . . . and missing.

They were getting into the *vibe* of the thing; making an effort.

Paradise said, 'Please, Mum.'

Summer said, 'I need absolute quiet.'

The women stopped humming. Even the candles behaved themselves and stopped spitting.

'Spirits, near and far,' Summer began, 'we have come to listen, to share in your wisdom. We are your friends, you are welcome.'

They started humming again, a little more in synch this

time. If they practised a little more, they might even find a tune. Maybe start a choir. That's what parents of a certain age did, didn't they? Or they knitted. Or they organised things for the community. Or they *somethinged*.

Beverley shivered. 'Oooh, Edith, I feel a chill.'

'I don't answer to that name any more,' Summer corrected.

'You're not at the ashram any more either,' Paradise said.

Beverly said, 'Sorry E- I mean, Summer.'

'Focus, ladies,' Summer said.

Slipping away from her mother, formerly known as Edith Compton-Barr, Paradise set about exploring what remained of grand old Livingstone Hall. Her eyes grew accustomed to the darkness as she came to the foot of the elegant staircase. Even in the low light, the decades of neglect were evident. Worn timbers, rotten wood, missing balustrades and a weird smell. Seasons of rain and damp were taking their toll on this forgotten corner of Gloucestershire.

Merely looking at those stairs filled Paradise with dread, so she darted past them to get to the ballroom.

A thrill stole through her as she walked through the paint-flaked archway, which opened out to the magnificent space. There was something so magical about a house being big enough and grand enough to hold balls. The people who must have danced here in a sumptuous time gone by.

The new moon shone no extra light; probably for the best as the signs of dilapidation broke Paradise's heart.

She slipped back down the hall and peered through a gap in the door to check on her mother and friends. They were doling out tarot cards now, turning them over one by one. Ah well, they weren't harming anyone, were they?

Leaving the women to their clairvoyant playdate, Paradise backed away and found herself at the foot of the stairs again.

'Maybe I can do this?' Tempting fate, she touched the first step with her left foot. Chills spread through her and she instantly pulled back and began walking the other way. The kitchen was where she needed to be anyway, at the other end of Livingstone Hall.

Careful to avoid the holes in the floor, she stepped in a zig-zag fashion. The damage looked worse here. The weather caused holes, allowing animals in, which continued the cycle of decay.

A familiar tapping came from a nearby window, sending a thrill of delight through her. It was a scullery, or dairy, or some kind of room used by servants. Paradise had never really understood what all the rooms were originally for. Now they were home to squatters and tramps in summer and miserably cold animals in winter.

Paradise turned to the window and looked into the face of a young gentleman. With a whisper of delight she said, 'Freddy, you're here!' Then she lifted the window sash to let him in.

'It's the new moon, isn't it?' He climbed through and wrapped his arms around her. 'Wouldn't miss it for the world.'

His heavily starched shirtfront puckered under the onslaught of their embrace. Fibres from Paradise's green mohair sweater tangled with his buttons as they snuggled.

The ruins of the old house floated away in her imagination as delicious, vibrant kisses filled Paradise with joy. Absorbed in her own little universe, she luxuriated in the perfect bubble made for just the two of them. It may have been cold and dark, but Freddy always brought dazzling warmth and light into her life.

Once they'd thoroughly completed their greeting, they set about exploring the dark old building.

'My dear, I do believe I hear music,' Freddy said, 'It would be most remiss if I did not beg of you one dance.'

'Then let's hit the disco.'

As they entered the ballroom, the decay of neglect fell away, replaced with imagined grandeur. A quartet played in the corner, a chandelier sparkled above, beautifully turned out couples waltzed around the room in perfect symmetry. Gentlemen in vintage suits and white ties; ladies in graceful gowns, tiaras and pearls.

It was so easy to pretend, now she had Freddy by her side, that she wore an elegant ballgown of the finest . . . well, whatever material they made ball gowns from. Something a lot more flowy than her orange corduroy skirt, heavy boots and long-sleeved green sweater. Her pretend dress floated diaphanously about her legs as Freddy led her through the turns. A little more imagination and he too changed from his footman attire into a form-fitting tuxedo and shiny black shoes.

When their lovely dance finished, the chandelier dimmed, the other dancers melted away and she and Freddy held each other. More kisses followed, because although dancing with Freddy was utterly wonderful, their time together was limited. When her mother and her friends packed up, he'd leave her.

As they left the ballroom, they checked on her mother's progress.

'She has new hair, I see?' Freddy said.

'It's called a lavender rinse.'

'Suits her.'

'You're so sweet.' Paradise said. 'I should give it a try myself.'

'Your hair is perfect,' Freddy said, twirling a long tress in his fingers. 'Don't ever change it.'

Paradise could have swooned, but she'd already seen what stage her mother and her friends were up to. 'We only have a little time left, they're on the teacups already.'

The women were pouring tea from an insulated flask, eight cups for the four of them.

'Just one cup, dear,' Miranda said. 'I don't seem to be able to hold on as long as I used to.'

'But Miranda, the first cup is for the present and the second is the future,' her mother protested.

'Then somebody better see some decent plumbing getting installed here in the very near future.'

'I use the bushes,' Christine said.

Definitely time to leave them to it, Paradise thought, as she took Freddy's hand and drew him into the library. The bookshelves were empty, just like the rest of the house, but their imagination soon filled it with books from floor to ceiling. Plump, leather-bound sofas appeared near the fireplace. Then the mantle repaired, the peeling wallpaper renewed and the windows were dressed with curtains and sashes.

'And a nice cosy fire for us to snuggle,' Freddy said. They sat before its glow. 'I do so look forward to our time together,' Freddy said.

'Me too,' Paradise said. 'But it's always so short.'

'True, although we do manage to achieve a great deal. Dancing, redecorating, not to mention the frequent stops for beautiful kisses.'

'Like this?' She turned her face towards him and pressed her lips to his.

A little while later he said, 'Oh yes.'

More beautiful kisses ensued, just the way Paradise liked them.

Suddenly Freddy pulled away. 'Something's wrong.'

'What's happening?' Hope drained from Paradise like water down a plughole as Freddy dissolved in front of her eyes. 'Don't go!'

He cried, 'She's sending me back!' as he vanished.

'It's too early!' Paradise cried to the now empty room. A few minutes ago, they were surrounded with sumptuous furnishings and a warm fire. Now she sat alone, on the warped floorboards of a faded room. The fireplace lay cold and unused for decades. The previous crackling of firewood replaced with the sound of women packing up in the room next door.

Paradise charged in and screamed at her mother, 'Why did you send him away?'

Summer slid the cards into their box and sighed. 'I guess a part of me always thought it would work one day.'

'It *was* working,' Paradise protested. 'It was working great! You really are psychic, Mum, you can really do this!'

'If it softens the blow, I have enjoyed our visits,' Miranda said, then crossed one leg in front of the other as she held back a sneeze. 'Just, y'know, not the lack of facilities.'

'Mum, please, listen. You really are good at this. You just don't know it!' But her mother continued to pack up.

Christine returned with the empty thermos and offered it to Miranda. 'You can go in here if you're desperate.'

'I'll hold on.'

'Suit yourself.'

Paradise stamped her foot but they took no notice. 'You're impossible! The lot of you! The one tiny bit of fun I get to have and you're ruining it.' Frustration roared through her at the thought of her mother giving up entirely. No more psychic fun meant no more visits to Livingstone Hall and no more Freddy.

No way!

Charging from the room, Paradise ran to the staircase. Coldness poured through her; the stairs repelled her. She clenched her hands, gritted her teeth and charged up the steps.

The third step creaked woefully, but she had no time to examine it. Part of the way up, she opened her eyes just to make sure that she'd really done it. Then she tripped on the landing with a crashing thud.

'Did anyone hear that?' Christine asked from below.

'What dear?'

Paradise stomped her feet to make as much noise as possible. She'd congratulate herself on conquering her fear of the stairs later; she had a bigger fear to contend with – never seeing Freddy again.

She reached the upstairs bedroom, the one directly above where her mother and friends were packing up. Paradise stomped about, imitating a herd of angry elephants. Anything to make her mother believe she'd made contact with the other side. Then she flattened herself to the floor, listening for voices from below.

Beverley said, 'There it is again.'

Christine asked, 'What?'

Beverley again, 'I thought I heard something?'

Paradise bashed her fists on the boards to make a ruckus.

'Nobody move,' her mother said. 'Beverley stop for a moment, I want everyone to be completely still. Is there anybody else here in the house?'

Paradise bashed the floor twice.

From below, Miranda called out, 'One tap for no, two taps for yes.'

Paradise contemplated bashing the floor just once, but this was no time for jokes. If she didn't convince the women they'd made contact, they'd never come back. She bashed the floor twice.

'Quick, Ed-I mean Summer, set the board up.' Beverley said.

Paradise charged out of the room and made for the stairs. Terror turned her body to ice. Something about these stairs turned her guts to water. No time for fear, she had to make it down and join the women at the ouija board. She took a deep breath, grabbed what was left of the handrail and charged. Her hand slipped straight off the wood – the long mohair sleeve offering no purchase. She staggered and grabbed for anything to stop her fall as her legs gave way. Her bottom landed with a heavy thud on the step, then she kept falling, boom, boom, boom, boom all the way to the third last step, which creaked and groaned under her weight. It should have been incredibly painful, but there wasn't time for that. Pulling herself together, she crept back into the front room where the women had re-lit several candles and had the board set up.

The women each had a finger on the token. Paradise snuck between her mother and Beverley, squished her finger into place and pushed the token towards the word 'yes' in the top corner.

'Who moved that?' Summer demanded.

Paradise kept her face calm and shook her head. Nobody spoke.

Slowly, Paradise moved the token around the board. She managed to spell out, 'Fred'. It would have been 'Freddy' but this was taking longer than she thought.

Everyone took their hands away, so Paradise followed suit.

Beverley demanded, 'Who did that?'

Christine said, 'I swear I didn't do it.'

All eyes turned to Christine.

Summer said, 'Fred as in Fred your first husband?'

Damn. Frederick was one of Christine's husbands. Stupid common name.

The women put their fingers on the token again and called for Christine's late husband to make himself known.

Paradise walked out of the room. The chance of ever seeing her Freddy again slipping through her fingers.

'Bravo!' A familiar voice said.

'Freddy!' There he was standing at the bottom of the stairs. She ran and embraced him, as if this might be her very last chance. 'I thought I'd ruined it all, that they'd called the wrong person, but I got it right!'

'Yes and no,' he said as they walked arm in arm towards the gap in the door to check on the women. 'It doesn't really matter who they called, it's more the *vibe* of the thing, as your mother says.'

Paradise squeezed him extra hard with love. 'They'll still pack up at some point tonight.' She sighed.

'That is inevitable. But you did brilliantly. Now they've had a taste of success, I'm sure they'll be back on a regular basis.'

'You're sure?'

'Quite sure.'

Paradise wrinkled her nose. 'How do you know?'

Freddy smiled, 'Because I'm psychic, don't you know?' Then he kissed her again, properly this time.

Nearly an hour later, as the night closed in, Summer Tourmaline and her friends packed up their belongings. Miranda came in from outside with a much more relaxed expression and helped stack things into baskets.

'This is our best visit yet,' Summer declared as she wrapped the board in an old pillowslip. 'I can't believe I came so close to giving up.'

Paradise sighed. 'You did good, Mum.'

'Same time next month?' Beverley asked.

'Definitely,' Christine said with a giggle. 'I'll bring a photo of Frederick next time. Might help us make better contact.'

'Good idea,' Summer said.

'We should all bring pictures next time,' Beverley said.

'What if we get really good at having a séance and they all turn up?' Christine asked.

'That's a worry,' Beverley said, 'You have outlived so many husbands.'

'I'd hardly call three 'so many',' Christine said.

Miranda turned to Summer, 'Are you all right?'

'Just a little sad, that's all.' Summer sniffed and blinked rapidly. 'The pictures at home are covered in dust. I can't bear to touch them.'

Uh, oh, Paradise knew that look. The stoic one her mother borrowed for such occasions.

'We'll get there,' Beverley gave Summer a warm hug. 'We had a breakthrough this time.'

'If it helps, I think you did really well too,' Paradise said.

'Thanks,' Mum said. 'It just gets so hard to keep going sometimes.'

'We'll get there,' Beverley repeated as they merged into a four-way hug.

Paradise stepped back to allow the women their moment. She wiped her cheek, but there was nothing on her finger when she pulled it away, just an echo of tears that used to come.

Summer stepped out of the hug and wiped away a very real tear on her face. 'I should be happy that we made progress, so why do I feel so sad?'

'Bittersweet memories,' Miranda said.

'We'll always be here for you,' Christine said, speaking for everyone.

Paradise said. 'I'll always be here too, Mum. You know I'm right here.'

It took only a few minutes for the four women to remove the last traces of their activities from Livingstone Hall.

From the window, Paradise waved them off. 'See you next month,' she said to the car's tail lights. 'I'll be right here, waiting.' A deep sigh rolled through her. Twenty-nine days of solitude until she could see Freddy again, and her mother, and her hippy dippy friends.

She'd cope. She'd manage somehow.

Turning, Paradise beamed with delight. There was Freddy, waiting for her. He was standing beside new people. No, wait, they weren't people, they only used to be people.

Now they were ghosts, just like her.

After she and Freddy embraced again, she looked to the others. 'Where did you two come from?'

There was a short skinny boy, who looked like he could be

Oliver Twist in a village play. Beside him was a tall older man, wearing a butler's suit from around Freddy's era.

He made a polite bow. 'I am Hector, at your service Miss . . . ?'

'Compton-Barr,' she held out her hand to shake his, 'Paradise Compton-Barr.'

'That explains it,' he shook her hand in greeting. 'Your form is strong, because of your connection to the family.'

Paradise shrugged. 'I guess so. How many more of you are there? I can hear faint voices. And . . . it sounds like there's a horse in the attic.'

TIMELESS TRADITION : SARAH J WOLFE

*T*he trouble with traditions passed down over umpteen generations is that someone has to be the person who carries them on. Even when they only happen once every century, if that. You only have one chance to get it right.

The responsibility weighs heavily on my shoulders. That's a figure of speech, by the way. Ghosts can't feel burdens physically. I am Hector, Head of Ghosts at Livingstone Hall. Before my fatal accident in 1862 I was the butler, so I am well suited to this position though, I should add, it took a number of years for others to realise that. Anyway, this is not about me.

Some say Livingstone Hall is the most haunted house in England. That may be true or it may not. But there are 472 - or 473 - of us, depending on how you count the headless horseman. (His head insists it be counted separately.) The previous three Heads of Ghosts didn't have to face this task at all. It's sheer bad luck for me that it has fallen during my term of office. You may be wondering what it is I have to do? I only have to preserve the future of the entire household of ghosts. That's all.

Our very existence – or non-existence – depends on what happens today. According to the legend set down in The Book, everything hinges on my ability to make two people fall in love; completely totally, irrevocably and immediately. There is no compromise on this. It has been an unbroken chain for the owners of this land since time immemorial. We'll know if I've succeeded by dinner time.

I was making a final check of the instructions in the leather-bound volume on the desk before me in the library when I heard the throaty roar of an expensive sports car on the forecourt of the Hall. It was time. I'd read the section that related to today's activities so many times I could recite it in my sleep. If I slept, which of course . . . I don't. Another figure of speech.

And all I have to help me in this endeavour is one thoroughly unreliable child ghost

'Do you have the pendant?'

Little Timmy held up the beautifully wrought pendant. It had been given to a Belgae princess by her lover and featured two golden dragons, studded with semi-precious stones and entwined together for time and all eternity. All we needed was for both of today's unsuspecting lovers to touch it at the right time and we would be safe.

'You know what to do?' I couldn't help asking Little Timmy for the ninety-billionth time.

Little Timmy rolled his eyes as only an eternally nine-year-old could do. He may look like a cherub in his Edwardian lace and dark blue velvet, but he is an irredeemable brat most of the time. Whilst I don't countenance violence, you can see why he died so young. As Head of Ghosts it falls to me to keep him in line, and I can't say it's an easy task, but no one else can pick pockets like him and that was what was needed now. If he would just do as he was told for once.

At least he has some stake in this. It's his future too.

'Car keys. Pendant.' Little Timmy recited and smirked. He truly was a cocky varmint, but needs must. The more nervous I got, the more irritatingly smug he became.

I nodded. 'All right, he's here. See you in the hall' and together we vanished from the library with a soft pop. Of course, when I reappeared in the hall, there was no sign of Little Timmy. As I said before, he's not that reliable.

Martha Compton-Barr hauled the dark wood door open to greet the visitor. The blasted thing had dropped on its rusty hinges and screeched like the proverbial banshee. Not for the first time she cursed her grandfather who had refused to make any repairs, in denial about the urgent need for them. But it was probably not a good greeting for the man who had come to buy the old place.

Martha put on her best smile, hoping it would disguise the anxiety that coursed through her. This man was here on behalf of a hotel entrepreneur who was expanding his chain of luxury country house hotels and theirs had been the only offer in six months. Not surprisingly, everyone else had looked at the condition of the place and run away.

Best foot forward and all that, she told herself. Why her grandfather had bequeathed her this tumbledown, ramshackle, semi-ruin of a Jacobean mansion she could only guess. He probably had the romantic idea that she would renovate it and Compton-Barrs would live here for another nine generations. As if. The house was saddled with more debts than any person ought to be allowed to have if they wanted to stay sane. There was no choice but to sell and soon before the bank foreclosed.

'Mr. Anderson, welcome to Livingstone Hall.' Martha held out her hand, while trying to hide her surprise. She had been expecting a crusty, old land agent, not Mr. Tall, Dark and Handsome, with a chiselled chin and fine blue eyes.

Joe Anderson ducked his head under the lintel of the stone doorway, his gaze flicking to the dust and cobwebs, and the frayed tapestries hung on the dull oak-panelled walls. Martha shifted uncomfortably, her hand still outstretched, the smile beginning to feel more like a grimace. Poor old Livingstone Hall had definitely seen better days but with the right new owner it could return to its former glory and she could be free. Please, he had to love it.

'Miss Compton-Barr,' He said as he finally shook her proffered hand. 'The house certainly has character.'

He could at least make that sound like a compliment. How could someone so gorgeous be so supercilious? Her palm buzzed where they had touched and a sharp pang of attraction hit deep in her stomach. She had to be careful not to react to him *in that way*. She wasn't on a date, she was here to sell a house.

Martha ushered him down the hall to the library where they settled into the dark red wing chairs by the empty fireplace. This was the cosiest room in the Hall, despite its grand proportions. The rhythmic ticking of the old clock on the mantelpiece somehow made it feel warm and welcoming. Martha scanned the room quickly. She'd moved all the good furniture into here and done her best to polish it to some semblance of a shine. It was certainly looking better than it had last week, but it also pointed out how dreadful the rest of the house was. As grandfather used to say, like putting lipstick on a pig.

Their chairs were separated by a low table where she'd

already placed the papers that Anderson's employer, the hotel person, had sent. She'd also prepared a silver tea tray with a large blue and white Wedgwood tea pot with matching cups and saucers, and a small plate of tiny sponge cakes.

'Thank you for coming Mr Anderson, but I fear your offer is rather lower than I had in mind,' she pressed her palms firmly into the arms of the chair to stop them shaking. The offer wouldn't cover the mortgages, never mind everything else that was owed. And it certainly didn't leave anything over for her to live on when she no longer had a home. If he thought she would be grateful for such a meagre offer, he was in for a nasty surprise.

'We appreciate that, Martha, and I have to say whilst the dry rot isn't as bad as we had thought,' he leaned forward and picked up the document with the bright red logo of the dry rot inspector, flicked through it and then slung it back onto the newly polished table, where it skidded to a halt next to the tea tray. 'There is still extensive work to be undertaken to bring this property up to the standards that a Boxell hotel is renowned for.'

Martha gritted her teeth, ready to do battle.

This wasn't going to plan. Time for me to get involved. I glided across the room and brushed the tips of my fingers across the top of Anderson's head. Just enough for him to feel as though a breeze had ruffled his hair.

Anderson furrowed his brow in such a way that his hard-chiselled good looks almost seemed cute. Almost. He ran his hand through his hair and leaned forward, both elbows on his thighs. 'Sorry, I know this may seem rude, but have we met before? You seem very familiar, but I can't place where?'

Excellent. The Anderson fellow had an intent look on his face.

Martha's gaze seemed riveted on the way his hair slid through his long narrow fingers. I appreciate some women have a soft spot for that almost jet black hair with a hint of a curl, though I have no idea why. My hair is . . . was . . . short and grey and just stands up straight. Anyway, as I said, this is not about me.

Martha cleared her throat and dragged her eyes back to his face. 'Hmmmm . . . yes. I'm thinking the same, but I can't put my finger on it either? Did you have a sister at Cheltenham Ladies College? Maybe we met at the sports?'

I'd done my homework on Anderson through the ghost concierge. He comes from a council estate in Leeds. Sister he may have, but I doubt his single mother could have afforded the fees to one of England's most exclusive private schools.

He flung himself back in his chair. His expression shifted abruptly, his face becoming still and his blue eyes losing their warmth. By all accounts he'd scrabbled his way up by his own hard work and cunning, and no doubt he was of the type who thought the daughter of an aristo had had it easy. Little he knew. Her grandmother's jewels and a set of Chippendale chairs had paid for her education. Just.

This wasn't going well enough. Nor fast enough. Time to do more than blow wind in their hair.

'There has been a home on this land since the Iron Age, Mr Anderson.' Martha's tones were clipped. 'This is a Grade II listed house and as your reports no doubt show, it needs completely rewiring and re-plumbing, the attics are full of bats and let's not talk about the last time we put the heating on. But it is in the heart of England and that has a high price tag.'

She paused to let her point sink in and then, unable to sit still, reached forward to the tea pot. She filled the two cups, then added milk and one sugar to Anderson's and handed it across the table to him.

As she did so, Joe Anderson's hand jolted as if something had jogged his elbow and in that instant their fingers touched.

A shiver ran down Martha's spine, a nice shiver, not the scary kind and her knees turned to water as the cup rattled in the saucer. Martha let go, bending her head on the pretence of picking up a small cake, her hair swinging forward to hide the heat rising to her cheeks.

She took a deep breath to steady herself, conscious of Joe Anderson's gaze fixed on her face. Something tickled her ear. Balancing her tea cup in one hand, Martha reached up to rub away the tickle.

By now I was whisking between the two chairs at a speed faster than a screaming poltergeist. I bent to whisper into Anderson's ear. So quietly that he might well think it was just a thought.

'Where will she go when you own this house?'

'When you sell the house . . .' he paused, almost as if he was surprised at himself, '. . . where will you go?'

Martha's face tightened.

Oh dear, she's not used to strangers asking such personal questions. Under normal circumstances it would have been none of his business. Too bad for Martha, today's circumstances called for anything but normal.

I glided across to Martha's side and whispered to her, *'Trust him.'*

She took a bite of the cake as she contemplated.

I tssked. Martha had a cake crumb stuck at the corner of her mouth but it seemed to have drawn Joe's attention away from her eyes. Yes! We are getting some breakthrough with Mr Icicle.

'Humour me.' Joe leaned forward and brushed the cake crumb away.

Martha froze, her eyes round. Her hand flew to her mouth.

Is it possible to have a surprised wolf? If it is, then Joe looked exactly like that. Grinning from ear to ear, but rather bashfully. And I didn't even have to prompt that one either. We're getting warmer, I think.

The skin where his rough fingertip had touched the corner of her lips hummed. Her mind turned into cotton wool. What was it she had to remember? Oh yes, not to respond to him *in that way*. Focus on selling the house.

Martha sat up straight. 'I shall follow the path of every daughter of a genteel family who has fallen on hard times and seek a position as a governess. These days, of course, that means going to Dubai or Moscow, but so be it. I have no illusions that I will find Mr Rochester, but I have to live somehow and of course the world thinks I've done nothing useful since leaving school.'

She forced herself to look him straight in the eye, terrified that he would laugh as others had done but Anderson just tipped his head to one side and asked, 'Have you? Done anything *useful*?'

'I've run this house without help for almost a decade, since before I left school. Managed the estate, with remarkably little money. Nursed my grandfather for seven years and believe me when I say he was a cantankerous old man. And I am remarkably adept at juggling the bills from the butcher, the baker and the candlestick maker whilst remaining on good terms with all of them.' She twisted her lips into a self-deprecatory smile. If felt good to finally say it out loud. 'Most people took it for granted that of course I would stay at home and nurse Grandfather whilst my parents remain in the Bahamas running up yet more debts.'

Joe contemplated her words. 'That doesn't sound like 'nothing useful'.'

'Nothing that *usefully* translates into a résumé that anyone wants'.

Anderson took a deep breath, tapping his fingertips on the arm of his chair and Martha began to regret her emotional blurt. Not impressed by her pathetic tale of woe? Or something else? This man gave every impression of having a heart of granite, but even granite could be carved into a beautiful shape if you have the right tools . . . and why had he brushed the corner of her mouth like that?

He cricked his neck as if trying to avoid someone or something breathing into his ear. 'Forgive me for saying this, but I can't possibly let a woman like you waste the rest of your life as a governess, Martha. I may well find myself in need of a . . .' He paused to contemplate his words. 'A housekeeper. For my London home. And an executive assistant.' He coughed. 'For my personal affairs.' He rumpled his forehead as if puzzled, and looked around the room. 'I'm sorry, I have no idea why I said that. It sounds positively Victorian.'

A huff of exasperation come from the direction of the fireplace, startling Martha.

~

One step forward, two steps back. Whilst The Book is an excellent guide, there are some damaged pages. Something to do with a bottle of claret and a lusty wench back in the time of Charles II. The information is unreadable now so what little we know has been passed on from one Head of Ghosts to another.

According to legend a Belgae princess ran away with a Roman legionnaire to get married in the temple of Mithras that was somewhere here about, probably under that vulgar Grecian pagoda by the lake. The Romans were heavily involved in subduing the Belgae at the time and they weren't exactly the best of friends. This was far, far worse than the Montagues and the Capulets.

The lovers were found at the temple and turned into mincemeat by their respective elders and betters. As they lay dying they vowed to be together for ever and ever. Corny? Yes, but that's the thing about true love. It often is.

In the temple, some magic happened and now Marcellus and Honbria meet, every hundred years or so, reincarnated in new lives, completely oblivious to their past and their destiny. They always meet here, on the land where they died.

Unfortunately for us ghosts, all of this true love comes at a cost, and this part has also been lost under the claret stains. All we know is that if this merry meeting does not result in immediate and irrevocable true love, then we, the ghosts, will become extinct. Not dead. That would be easy. We will be extinct. Gone completely from this world or the next. Of course, no one has actually tested this but there are signs that it's correct. You may have wondered where the other 472 (473) ghosts have been all day. The answer is they are now so weak and pale that they are unable to leave the attics. We are fuelled, quite literally, by the power of love and we've almost used it up.

I drummed my fingers on the mantelpiece. Where was Little Timmy? The Book clearly outlines the order of events and the brat was cutting it very fine. As if on cue, Little Timmy materialised beside me, giving me the fright of my ex-life.

His only responsibility today had been to remove Joe's car keys from his pocket and substitute the pendant. He should have picked Joe's pocket whilst he walked down the hall. Now the man was sitting down it would be so much harder. I raised my eyebrows at the annoying little ghost and all I got for my troubles was another irritating smirk and a flick of his hand towards a large Chinese urn sitting in the far corner of the room, by a stone mullioned window. I did my ghostly gliding over the red Indian patterned carpets and peered in. At the bottom was a shiny black car fob, bearing the distinctive Aston Martin logo.

Little Timmy swaggered over and whispered 'Got it off him in the driveway when he first arrived. You are so slow, old man.'

As you have gathered already, humans can hear us but most of them can't see us. So we tend to whisper when they're around. It scares the living daylights out of them to hear disembodied voices and we do not like to alarm our humans unduly, except when provoked

'And the pendant?' I hissed. He's really getting under my skin now.

'In his pocket, old man.' Little Timmy grinned.

I am getting rather tired of the 'old man' epithet, but as that was Little Timmy's work done I decided to let it pass. 'You can go now.' I dismissed him with my best imperious voice.

Except of course he didn't go. He just wandered back to the fireplace where he was eyeing the sponge cakes with all the glee of the average nine-year-old boy. Pointlessly, I might add, because ghosts can't eat.

The clock above the fireplace showed it was nearly 5pm. Assuming Anderson needed to get back to London this evening, things were moving too slowly. So far they'd drunk a cup of tea, eaten some cake and had a bit of a chat. If I was any judge of these things (and as a butler I pride myself on being able to read character) I'd say there is *some* attraction, but it's not exactly sizzling. There's a long way to go.

According to The Book, they are meant to be mesmerised

with each other by now. Their knees are almost touching, but they're still firmly sitting on their chairs. You can't have sizzling attraction from separate chairs!

In my head, I started running through all the instructions in The Book, of which there are many. Had I missed anything out?

1. Ensure that the modern day Marcellus can't leave in his chariot. Done.
2. Place Honbria's pendant where they can both find it at the right time. Done
3. Build mutual fascination.

That's where I'm stuck. The Book clearly outlines there are nine more steps to go through before ensuring they both hold the pendant. From what I could read under the wine stains, it's critically important to do this properly. We must do this by the book. My heart sank (or it would have if I'd still had one).

'This has been delightful, Martha, but I am afraid I do need these papers signed. I am expected back in London . . .' Joe glanced up at the clock on the mantle to underscore his point.

Martha's shoulders slumped.

I'd seen those same papers from the bank. To accept an offer that low would shackle her with debt for the rest of her life. But Comptor-Barrs are stronger than that. I whispered in her ear, 'There has to be a better offer'.

Martha nodded and put some steel into her spine. 'I can't accept this offer, Mr Anderson. It's just not enough.'

Frustration boiled inside my chest. This young woman had held everything together for years against all the odds and it came down to this sordid haggling over money.

'In that case, I regret . . .' Anderson started to rise, his hand going to his trouser pocket for his car key. Instead, thanks to

Little Timmy, it wasn't a key that Joe pulled out. It was Honbria's locket. He stared at it.

Martha's eyes widened as she rose from her chair and reached for it. 'Oh, it's beautiful,' she said, as had Honbria when Marcellus first gave it to her. Martha's fingers brushed the dragons in the ancient gold, nestled in the palm of his hand.

Too soon! Too soon! The magic isn't strong enough yet!

The Book is very clear. Everything must happen in the right order. Horror had me rooted to the spot.

Just as I thought things could get no worse, Little Timmy leapt forward to the fireplace and threw a tantrum as only he could. With one violent push, he swept the heavy wooden-cased clock off the mantle.

The clock flew towards Martha, bounced off the arm of her chair and crashed to the ground, catching the edge of the tiled hearth. Shards of glass flew in all directions. The wooden case splintered and the inner workings resounded in a phenomenal cacophony of boings and pings.

A sharp pain in her hand drew a yelp from Martha, who looked down to see a thin trail of blood where a splinter of glass had cut her finger. With an exclamation, Joe reached for her hand and inspected it, before folding it into his palm and drawing her into his embrace.

Martha looked into Joe Anderson's eyes. 'This is going to sound really odd ...'

'Try me.'

'When you walked through the door I thought I knew you. Not like we had met somewhere, but like I *really* knew you. I knew what you were thinking, what you would do next. Even how you like your tea.'

'I know . . .' Joe cocked his head to one side. 'Earlier, I asked if you would be my, err, housekeeper.'

Martha nodded, her heart beating so fast she was sure he must be able to hear it.

'I'd like to revise that.' He paused, holding her away from him so he could see her face clearly. 'Martha Compton-Barr, would you do me the honour of becoming my wife?'

"Yes . . . yes, I will. But first, will you kiss me?"

What just happened? I'm completely confused. The Book is clear. There are twelve steps to follow in order. They've leapt right over steps four to eleven. I turned to Little Timmy, who was grinning from ear to ear.

'You're so slow, old man.'

THE GREY LADY : ALISON STUART

'Oh dear, this can't be good,' Hector, Head of Ghosts, muttered.

A bright red Italian sports car, followed by a dark blue van swept around the bend of Livingstone Hall's weed-infested driveway. The sports car skidded to a stop outside the old house and the van drew up beside it.

For months, the spectral inhabitants had endured a circus of real estate agents, and potential buyers, traipsing through the house. A few had been dissuaded with judicial and strategic shoves in the back and unexplained tripping but nothing could deter the odious Herbert Boxell Junior the Third, or HBJ3 as he called himself.

A succession of architects and builders had crawled into every conceivable nook and cranny, shaking their heads about the dry rot, the state of the trusses, the death watch beetle and other structural issues. Even worse, blueprint plans had appeared on the library table waiting for perusal by HBJ3 and his minions.

Hector had reported to the other ghostly inhabitants about plans for roof top golf, an indoor swimming pool, a health spa, pedalos on the lake and even more alarmingly, a basement disco.

'That sounds rather fun,' Freddy and Paradise had agreed. The others just stared at them, and the White Lady moaned and dripped water.

While the attempts by the ghosts to deter HBJ3 had gone unregarded by the man, he seemed to take an unhealthy interest in them. Hector had overheard him asking the agents about the reputation of the hall as the 'most haunted house in England' and when assured that, yes indeed, there were numerous stories about the place being haunted, HBJ3 had responded by rubbing his hands together.

'Excellent,' he had said in a self-satisfied tone that had sent shivers down Hector's spectral spine

HBJ3 vaulted nimbly over the door of the sports car, as Lettice Chapman, the newly appointed manager of the Livingstone Hall Country House Hotel and Spa tottered on unsteady high heels out of the front door.

Hector's gravest fears were confirmed as he read the logo on the side of the van.

> *P.I.S.*
> *Paranormal Investigation Society*
> *You Haunt 'em. We Flaunt 'em'*

The driver opened the door and jumped down. A fit looking man in his late forties, he wore a tight black tee shirt with the PIS logo stretched across his chest, and GARY in bold letters on the back. He stood with his hands on his hips looking up at the house, while his well-drilled team began to unload equipment.

From his vantage point in the office window, Hector drew a deep breath. He had heard of the PIS through his unearthly concierge network. They were famous for a high-rating TV show called *Who's Living in Your Wainscot?* Hector had rather enjoyed watching television with the last resident of Livingstone Hall, but this had not been one of Martha's preferred shows. She had been rather partial to *Midsomer Murders*.

'You have free run of the place,' HBJ3 boomed. 'I just need some hard evidence that these so-called ghosts exist and the guests will come flocking in.' He nudged the skeletally thin Lettice in the ribs. 'Can't you see it, Lettice? Haunted house themed weekends. The Americans will love it. Hallowe'en will be huge. We'll have ghost hunting expeditions . . .'

Hector did not wait to hear any more. He turned sharply on his well-booted but ethereal foot and blew hard on the dog whistle that worked equally well on spectres and canines.

The 472 ghosts (or 473 if you counted the headless horseman's head separately) crowded into the attic, listening in appalled silence as Hector recounted the activity going on downstairs.

'Cool,' said Paradise. 'We could have some fun with that lot.'

Freddy raised his arms and wiggled his fingers. 'Whooooooo.'

'It is not cool,' Hector said. 'Do you really want to be turned into a tourist attraction with people armed with those electronic thingies poking at you all night?'

The ghosts murmured their disapproval. Chulhain, the Iron Age spectre, grunted and beat his spear on his shield.

'No,' Hector said. 'No violence. As long as the investigators are in the building, there is to be no ghostly activity, AT ALL. Understood? That includes you, Timmy.' He fixed the child ghost with a hard glare. 'Even if they produce one of those trays of cream buns.'

Timmy stuck out his lower lip. 'No fun,' he said.

'Absolutely no fun of any description. We just want these people gone without a skerrick of evidence that we exist. Are we agreed?'

A general murmur and nodding of ghostly heads signified assent. No ghost in his or her or its right mind wanted to be turned into a sideshow.

As Hector opened his mouth to issue further instructions, a stench somewhere between a three-week rotted corpse and the dankest cellar permeated the room. Even the bravest ghost shrank back against the wall as an entity materialised among them.

Some had described her as a grey mist, others as a woman in a tattered grey gown, her grey hair falling in unkempt tangles down her back. Others never lived to describe her at all. The sight of this apparition was said to have accounted for the deaths of several elderly retainers with weak hearts over the centuries.

The Grey Lady.

The most feared ghost in the Livingstone Hall ghostly family, The Grey Lady only appeared on very rare occasions – foretelling the violent death of the male heir to the family. Of enormous age, the only ghost who preceded her was Chulhain. The last time she had been seen was when Bertie Compton-Barr had died on the Somme in 1916. Bertie's brother had inherited the hall, and on his death, his granddaughter, Martha.

Hector rose to his spectral feet and swallowed. She turned her black, hollowed eyes on him. He thought she might have smiled, if the death's head grimace could be described as a smile.

'Always a pleasure, dear lady,' he said, 'but your timing is a little unfortunate. You see . . .'

Something like a roar, or a rush of wind emanated from her dark mouth.

'There are no male heirs to the Compton-Barrs,' Hector said in a rush. 'All dead.'

The Grey Lady cast him a malevolent glance, which, if he had still been alive, would probably have added him to the list of unfortunate elderly retainers. She glided, or possibly drifted, across to the window and raised her right arm, pointing with a skeletal finger at the blue van.

Hector frowned. Two young people were engaged in unloading equipment, a slight, young woman with short auburn hair. Her tee shirt declared her name to be Mel. The other, a young man, with unkempt blonde hair and an un-English tan was apparently called DANNY. Hector drew in a breath, or he would have done if he still breathed. There was no mistaking the Compton-Barr nose on the young man. Whoever he was, the last male heir to the Compton-Barrs had returned to Livingstone Hall, and if the Grey Lady's appearance was to be credited, he would not be leaving.

'Get a move on you two!' Gary Symes, the founder, CEO and consultant to the Paranormal Investigative Society shouted across the courtyard at Melody Peters and the newest member of the PIS, an Australian backpacker who had been introduced to the team as Danny Barr.

Melody cast the newcomer a furtive glance from under her heavy fringe. She'd not met many Australians, but having been raised on a steady diet of *Neighbours*, she found the proximity of a genuine Aussie, particularly one who looked like he would be more at home on a surf board than engaged in paranormal investigation, exciting. She had been rather looking forward to the opportunity of getting to know him better.

'So,' she braved conversation as he thrust a box into her outstretched arms, 'Where did Gary find you?'

Danny paused as he hauled the equipment out of the van. He scratched his fashionably stubbled chin. 'Saw the ad and thought it would be a bit of laugh. What about you?'

Melody hesitated. 'I find paranormal investigation a very serious business,' she said.

'You don't actually believe in them, do you?' Danny scoffed.

Melody glanced up at the house. Believe in them? She could already sense the presence of more than one entity. Many more than one . . .

'There are things I have seen that can't be explained,' she mumbled.

'I think that's it.' Danny surveyed the back of the van. 'Where are we setting up?'

'In the library,' Melody said from over the top of the boxes.

As she stepped over the threshold, the voices in her head started. How many entities lived here? If even a couple were about tonight then Mr. Boxell would be very pleased with the PIS report at the end of the investigation.

Gary's technicians scurried around setting up the digital cameras, sound recorders, EMF sensors and videos, all linked back to the array of computer equipment on the far end of the long library table.

HBJ3 watched the activity from a position by the fireplace, a self-satisfied smirk on his tanned face. Lettice Chapman, handed around cups of tea and plates of sandwiches.

'I really hope they don't find anything,' she confided in Melody, while casting nervous glances around the rapidly darkening room.

'Why? Do you think we might?' Melody asked.

Lettice swallowed. 'My mother always said I had an

overactive imagination, but I could swear I saw a gentleman in an old-fashioned tweed suit standing in my office, but don't tell Mr. Boxell.'

'I won't,' Melody promised.

Gary gathered the team together and split them into pairs.

'Melody, Danny; I want you to take the ballroom, sitting room, snooker room and principal staircase area.'

A tingle of anticipation ran down Melody's spine, not so much from the prospect of what the night might bring, but the thought of having Danny's company all to herself.

Armed with control objects, portable EMF readers and ghostly gadgets, the team dispersed to their appointed corners of the house as Gary settled down in front of the computer screens with HBJ3 beside him to monitor the night's activities. Lettice excused herself and retired to the newly constructed staff quarters in the stable yard.

Hector watched the activity, noting with some relief that his own preferred haunt, the manager's office, had not been subjected to the installation of the preposterous machinery. Leaving the other ghosts to skulk in the furthest corners of the attic, he retired to his favourite chair to consider what to do about The Grey Lady. Just as he settled into the soft, worn leather the house plunged into darkness.

The door opened with the faintest click. The young woman Hector had seen unloading equipment entered the darkened room. Hector froze. Too late to dematerialise, she had seen him. She was looking straight at him. A sensitive. He had come across them before. It wouldn't matter how well the ghosts hid, this girl would know they were there.

'Good evening,' she said. 'Which one are you?'

Hector cleared his throat. 'Hector, Head of Ghosts. Your servant, ma'am. And you are?'

'Melody Peters. My apologies for startling you. Miss Chapman said she had seen you in her office so I thought it would be a good place to start.'

Hector sunk into the chair and buried his head in his hands. 'I know what that awful man wants to do with us. We are doomed.'

'Not necessarily.' She glanced around the room. 'Gary didn't think to put anything in this room, so no one else knows you are here. Where are the others?'

Hector ignored the question, seeing in this fragile slip of a human, the only chance the ghosts had to save their collective dignity.

'We have a problem, Miss Peters. One of your number is the last male heir of the Compton-Barrs and he is about to die violently.'

Melody stared. 'What do you mean?'

'The Grey Lady is here.' Hector said and went on to explain, as best he could, the fearful apparition.

'But . . . but . . . ' Melody had gone as pale as . . . a ghost. 'How can we save him? '

'Forget Barr . . . what are we going to do if the Grey Lady shows herself?'

Melody and Hector, Head of Ghosts, stared at each other.

Melody found Danny in the ballroom, studying his EMF. He huffed out a sigh. 'This is just boring,' he said. 'Not a flicker.'

Melody looked at his bent head. 'Did you know Barr was the surname of the family that used to own Livingstone Hall? The Compton-Barrs.'

He looked up, his face unreadable in the gloaming. 'My

Dad was a Compton-Barr. Told me his great grandad was sent to the colonies in disgrace. He dropped the hyphen.'

'So, you are the last male heir of the Compton-Barrs?' Melody said more to herself than to him.

Danny shrugged. 'I suppose so. I don't have a brother and all my cousins are girls.'

Melody glanced around the ballroom. There didn't seem to be anything here to cause Danny any harm. They would be fine as long as they stayed here. Perhaps Hector was imagining things? If it was possible for ghosts to have an imagination.

Danny pocketed his EMF and headed for the door. 'I've had enough of this. I'm going up to the roof,' he said.

'There are no ghosts up there,' Melody almost shrieked.

Danny shrugged. 'The moon's up. It's a beautiful night. I want to see the view.'

Melody lunged for him and missed. He was gone, loping toward the principal staircase, taking the stairs two at a time. Melody followed, cursing her neglected gym membership as her lack of fitness began to tell on the stairs.

They burst out on to the roof and for a moment, Melody had to agree it could not have been a more perfect night. A cold, bright moon rose high in a midnight blue sky, casting a silver shadow along the line of poplars leading to a distant lake and beyond that a small round Grecian temple. Above the tree tops, a ruined tower cut into the sky, the last remnant of an older structure, built for a more violent time but now part of the garden landscape. It made for a perfect vista envisioned by a long dead architect, Melody thought. In other circumstances, it would be the ideal setting for a bit of romantic 'getting to know you', but tonight it was possibly the most dangerous place in the house for Danny to be.

Danny caught her hand. 'You see, Mel? This is heaps better than muddling around looking for stupid ghosts.'

He caught her hand and drew her along a narrow walkway.

The slated roof rose steeply on one side. A low raised parapet acted as a barrier between them and a long fall to the driveway.

A long fall . . . a violent death.

Melody pulled her hand free. 'We've got to go back, Danny. It's not safe up here.'

'Safe as houses.'

As he spoke a grey mist rose from nowhere, circling icy tentacles around their bodies, A vile stench overwhelmed them. Melody clutched Danny's arm. 'Come back, Danny. Now!'

He hesitated for a second before relenting. They turned back to the narrow doorway with Melody leading the way.

Between them and the safety of the door, the freezing mist transformed into the shadowy form of a woman in a long, ragged habit. Her face a death's head smirked beneath hanks of rotting grey hair. Melody's breath caught. She had never seen or sensed anything as terrifying in her life.

The spectre raised her right hand and pointed a skeletal finger directly at Danny.

'What the . . . is that?' Danny said.

That is your death, Melody thought.

'His death,' the apparition echoed in her mind.

'Good. We can communicate,' Melody replied.

Melody held out her left arm behind her, as if to shield Danny from toppling over the edge of the roof. 'Don't move, Danny. Not a muscle.'

She raised her right hand like a traffic warden.

'No. He's not yours.' Melody's chest tightened as her words entered the essence of the Grey Lady. *'The Compton-Barrs are all dead.'*

'Not this one. He will die tonight,' the lady whispered.

'Why?'

'It is his time. It is his fate . . .'

'Nothing is certain,' Melody replied. *'Go in peace, Grey Lady.*

Let this one live. If he dies, that will be the end of Livingstone Hall. You will be hunted to every corner of this house by . . . ' she struggled to find a word that the entity would understand. *'By witch hunters and exorcists and tourists with cameras. You will never know peace. Go back to your grave, Grey Lady and rest.'*

The grey mist shimmered in the moonlight. 'Witch hunters? Exorcists?' And in one long shuddering breath, 'Tourists?'

'What price is this man's life?'

The Grey Lady sighed, her breath coming straight from hell. 'I am too old for this modern world. Keep him.'

The mist dissipated, drawing the foul stench away with it.

Danny staggered back against the slope of the roof, dislodging several tiles that cracked and broke on the walkway. He swore, adding a few choice words that Melody assumed were Australian, and unflattering, in origin.

'Do you still not believe in ghosts?' she said, sitting down beside him.

He wiped a hand over his forehead.

'What . . . what did it want?'

'You. Apparently, you are the last male heir of the Compton-Barrs and . . .' she glanced around her. 'And do you mind if we get down off here and I'll explain it all but I really don't feel safe.'

Danny stood up and took a step. A piece of broken tile caught under his foot and he slipped, swaying precariously on the narrow walkway. His feet went from under him and all Melody could do was watch, as if in slow motion he swayed toward the edge of the roof. He poised there for what seemed like an eternity, his limbs flailing as he tried to regain his balance.

'You can't play with fate.' A whisper, overlaid with the stench of death, sighed into Melody's ear.

A rush of cold air blasted past Melody. Danny started to fall forward, twisting and wrenching as he appeared to hurl himself against the safety of the tiles.

An unearthly howl echoed up to the stars.

Danny lay against the roof staring up at the velvet darkness, his breath coming in short gasps.

'Something grabbed me. Stopped me falling . . .' he said. 'I think I need a stiff drink,' he added.

Melody leaned against the door frame, waiting for her heartbeat to return to normal, and wondered if it were possible to high five the large Iron Age warrior drifting past her.

Hector, Head of Ghosts, whispered in her ear. 'Well done, Miss Peters. I doubt we will see The Grey Lady again.'

As they regained the security and solidity of the staircase, Melody turned to Danny.

'Please, Danny. Not a word to Gary or anyone about what happened up there.'

He stared back at her. 'You've got to be kidding. Who would believe me anyway?'

'I'm sorry that I have nothing to report,' Gary concluded the round up briefing with HBJ3 the next morning. 'It was a completely uneventful night.'

Leaning against the bookshelves in the library, Melody and Danny exchanged a quick glance. Over by the fireplace, Hector, Head of Ghosts, punched the air.

'No ghosts at Livingstone Hall?' HBJ3's mouth turned down at the corners. 'Oh well, we'll just have to work on that rooftop driving range.'

HERO OF THE DISH : ELIZA RENTON

*V*ictor Lye sat at a table for one in Livingston Hall's recently renovated dining room. The light from the window drowning in his ash grey suit. Another acid review percolated behind glasses too big for his face. Lye deserved a taste of his own medicine, and Pomegranate Green would provide. She sashayed to his table, his just desserts, shrouded in whipped cream, held high.

One bite landed Pomegranate a lifetime sentence for murder with intent. Clawing at his throat, arms akimbo, her nemesis tumbled backwards to the floor.

'Argh, the bitch poisoned me.'

Bored by the whole spectacle, Hector, Head of Ghosts, poured the Lady in White another champagne cocktail. It amused him to see her tiddly.

Lye, coughed and spat, white bubbly froth erupting from his mouth.

Hector looked unimpressed. 'Pom, what on earth have you done this time?'

'I didn't mean to kill him. He's supposed to suffer a little and groan his way to bed.'

'Do something, before he screams his way to a coffin.'

'Er ... um ...

Bring health to his body

Heal mind and soul too.

Strength and well-being

Make it all new.

Fishcakes!'

Pom muttered the spell over Victor Lye's twitching body. Resigned to this demon staying dead, she barely dodged Lye's hands as they flew at her throat.

Hector sprang from behind the bar and shoved Pom towards her kitchen. 'Get lost, Pom. Now.'

Within hours, Lye's venomous review struck the pages of *Greatest Gourmet*.

Slamming a ticket to the Paranormal Investigator's Conference in Vietnam into her hand, Hector ordered Pom's bags packed. So much for keeping her job, staying with family.

'Take a break Pom.'

Hector's message clear, get her head together or embrace early retirement.

Saigon's *Majestic Hotel* teemed with witches. Pom's session, *Quick Ways to Spot a Ghost in an Everyday Pot Plant*, delivered without hiccups. Time to retire to the bar.

'Mai Tai, please. Don't skimp on the smoky almonds, love.' Pom hitched her red, pencil skirt mid-thigh, and perched a luscious hip over a bar stool. The bartender winked.

In the foyer, a noisy group of tourists bustled around a chirpy tour guide. His yellow flag held high. 'Everyone for the afternoon tour to Cu Chi, follow me.' He pinned a questioning look her way.

'Are you with us?'

Me? Heck, why not? It was a bit early to drink, even if oblivion had its merit. Pom snatched a handful of nuts, hooked her bag over her shoulder, and hurried after the sightseers entangled in the revolving door.

Content to keep her distance from fellow tourists, Pom secured her headphones and settled in for a nap. Damn playlist needed an edit, reminders of Mick flooded her blood. It had been a long six months since he'd dumped her and moved on.

As the bus came to a stop, a boy, sitting next to her, pierced her eardrum with his shriek of delight.

'Bang . . . bang. Awesome! Cu Chi Tunnels.'

A war memorial, awesome, not. Everywhere, the smell of death and dust. Danh waited at the entrance, the eyes of a demented fox terrier, counting each descending tourist.

'Hurry, hurry, there's lots to see.'

Damp, fetid air cloyed at Pom's lungs and swelled under her skin. Difficult to imagine how the legendary Tunnel Rats coped? A moan echoed ahead. Someone must have tripped in the dark tunnel. The third time it happened, she knew. Damn ghost. Retreat.

Pom sat on the log, a soggy rice paper roll leaking into her lap. A half hour before the bus returned to the hotel and food options were limited in the tourist trap. A short distance away, Danh encouraged the still shrieking boy to climb the relic of the M41 tank. The long gun focussed on the crowd. *'Exterminate, obliterate, annihilate.'*

Choking on her soggy spring roll, a lump lodged deep in Pom's throat. Tears simmered behind her eyeballs. Pathetic.

Fu . . . freckles! The ghost emerged from the tunnel, a woman beside him. She wore no hat in the midday sun; a child clutched the hem of her skirt. Pom sniffed, shifted her sunglasses to the bridge of her nose, and peered at the unmistakable beauty of the ghost, an American soldier. Late afternoon sun glinted from the buttons on his uniform as he raised the crying child onto his shoulders. The Flying Angel giggled. The soldier smiled.

Phew! A narrow escape. Safe in the bar of the Majestic, Pom settled into her second drink, curious to hear more about the Cu Chi Tunnel Rats.

'Brave men . . . during the Vietnam War, the American Rats ferreted the Viet Cong from their underground hideout . . . treacherous work.' The bartender's conversation drifted to well-worn pick-up lines. Very cute; a third Mai Tai not a great idea. Pom tipped him and toddled off to the Ben Thanh Night Market. Serious shopping in mind.

The balmy evening, charged with delightful aromas of fish and chilli, enveloped animated vendors haggling with keen buyers. Pom's fingers stroked the silk scarf draped around her neck, the one Mick had bought her, the last time she was here. Nothing like a living ghost to screw with the brain.

On cue, the soldier appeared from behind purple silk floating in the breeze. Once seen, never forgotten; romantics describe it as 'love at first sight'. The air shifted, whistled new path ahead. No turn-off, stop or delay, the gate opens to endless distraction. *Shoot me dead!* Doomed, would she ever be free of ghosts, living or otherwise?

Two long, limber strides and he was at her side; his grip on her elbow firm, insistent. He murmured close to her ear.

'Come with me.' Not a request.

'Excuse me, what do you think you're doing?' Soldiers– arrogant alphas the lot of them.

'We have to talk. I need access to *my* world, *your* world.' Hooked to his bulging bicep, they sidled along a dark alley, stopping before a metal door guarded by a gorilla. Neon lighting flashed above the entrance, Lush Bar.

'*No frigging way*, I'm not going in there.'

'Take it easy.' What a voice, smooth as honey on hot, buttered crumpets.

Pom tore her arm from the soldier and grabbed his hand.

'Come with me. My hotel's nearby. There's a bar; we can talk.' Sparks from their entwined fingers illuminated the shadows in the alley.

'What are you drinking?' Not interested in his reply, Pom returned with a Budweiser and a harmless lemonade.

'A Bud?' He looked hurt. 'What's your name, honey?'

Not honey! 'Pomegranate Green . . . Pom.'

A crooked smile blossomed beneath gentle brown eyes, the colour of rich chocolate. Teeth so white they belonged in a jar. 'Good to meet you, Pom, I'm Apollo Kingdom.'

Waving away his outstretched hand, she cut him dead. 'This isn't a date, buster.'

He took a swig of his Bud; his eyes dashed all over her, uncomfortable, intoxicating. 'You're her . . . aren't you?'

'Her?'

'The paranormal investigator? I've been expecting you.'

'You have?' Time to make a call; Hector better pick up.

'What's that?' Apollo stared at her mobile phone.

'Magic.' Her patience, thin; the traitor answered on the second ring.

'Hector, you son of a . . . I require an Angel Flight, routine retrieve, and dispatch; as if you didn't know? I can't believe you banished me here and didn't clue me in . . .'

Hector coughed, interrupting her rant. 'Pomegranate, you've been a misery, ever since Mick left. You needed something to take your mind off things. Besides, If I'd told you, you wouldn't have gone.'

'Damn right. I've done my fair share of warriors, searching for a way home. It takes a lot out of a girl.' Her ghost swallowed and lowered his eyes to the floor.

Transport secured, Pom headed for the portal, Apollo Kingdom in her wake. 'Time to go.'

On edge since their return to the Hall, when had the threat of the monthly curse ever signalled so far ahead? Excuses Pom. No curse mashed with her head or flipped pancakes in her stomach. One military ghoul challenged her principles and questioned her *fey*-dar.

For the past month, he'd stuck by her side, refusing to mingle with the others. Yesterday, she'd caught herself looking for him. He made her laugh, chilled her self-talk, lightened her heart.

Finished for the evening, Pom took a moment before joining the party. Apollo would pass over soon. Leave. Safe in her kitchen pans crashed, plates flew. The only solace found in a cocktail of Pimms and music. Alcohol with a dash of poetry, laced with melody, never failed to trump the dread of relationships.

Was it wise to swap the steel caps for killer heels? Her little toe burned against the pressure of her Docs. Yep! Pom looked in the mirror and fluttered her eyelashes, the delicate silk of her Valentino Wrap dress tickled her knees.

The Lady in White's birthday cake iced, time to let loose and enjoy herself. A swig of the cooking sherry and a quick slash of cherry bomb lipstick. *Ready!* The doors to the kitchen swung open. Her feet clicked a steady rhythm over the marble floor leading to the music room.

Livingstone Hall wore candlelight well, illuminating the laughter in everyone's eyes. Lively voices and joyful laughter could be heard a mile away. Apollo stood at the piano, a cheap tuxedo, borrowed from Hector, hung like Armani from his athletic frame and graceful lines.

The Lady in White smiled only for the handsome soldier as she began to play. Lost in his song, Apollo's eyes never left Pom; his bewitching look sent goosebumps chasing along her arms. *Too much cooking sherry.*

Apollo's rich baritone voice rocked Pom's bones. The last notes of the tune died away, and her earlier chagrin returned. Unable to bear the knowing in his gaze, Pom bolted.

She hid in the veggie garden, surrounded by a cape of rose-scented geraniums, jasmine and turnips. Apollo's chest brushed against her back. He'd found her. Strong hands rested on her shoulders with a tenderness that said *you were missed.*

'You left in a hurry, sugar. Didn't you like my song?'

Unable to move, her hands hung rigidly by her side.

'What happened, Apollo?'

'You mean, how did I get dead?'

'I guess.'

'I'd like to tell you I'm a hero, took bullets for my buddies.'

'But . . .'

'A two-step bit me.'

'A two-step? For God's sake, what's that?'

'A deadly snake. Capt'n persuaded me to use a gas mask. VC loved using the stuff. The mask messed with my side vision; I didn't see the snake until it was too late.'

'By all things idiotic . . .' Big mouth. Pom blushed, her hair on fire.

'No argument there.'

'Sorry. I didn't mean to be crass. But, why are you hanging around? You should have passed over by now.'

'No can do, honey. I have something that belongs to Eula.'

'Eula? Who's she?'

'She's been my girl since school. A ring. I have her engagement ring. I was gonna propose on my next leave.'

'Ah. You've lost your girlfriend?' Stuff was beginning to make sense.

'That's right, she moved to London.' Over fifty years ago. She'd be dribbling in the old folks' home by now.

'Is that it? That's all that's keeping you here?' She hoped he was hanging back for her. *Get a grip, Pom, he's a ghost, a dead man!* Pom slammed her hands on her thighs and turned to face him. 'Thank fairy cakes.'

'S'cuse me?'

'This will be a piece of cake.'

'Really?'

'Yep.' The ground shifted to blancmange beneath her feet. Resting her palms against Apollo's chest, she tried to steady herself. Of course, a girl, some other girl. Wandering soldiers were infinitely predictable.

∿

'Wait. Don't go, not yet.' Apollo caught Pom's wrist and held on. Had she felt it too? The tingling?

Since Cu Chi, the life in this woman ate at past worlds causing them to fall away. Her full lips, enticing, her smoky blue eyes compelling. Each breath tickled the end of his nose as their lips met and he sank into the luxury of her plush, wet kiss.

For a few seconds, she swayed in front of him, her eyes closed, her breath held.

'Wow! What was that for?'

Truth? He wasn't sure. More than gratitude. Something similar to peace. *Oorah!*

'Thank you.'

'Er . . . No sweat.'

∿

Once Pomegranate Green was on the case, it seldom took long

to wrap it up. Known for her magical prowess and inquiry skills she'd earned the rank of Paranormal Investigator Extraordinaire. She'd located Eula, surprisingly still *compos mentis*, in Hampstead, a retirement village close to the Heath.

Apollo was in the music room. Hand on hip, Pom, flicked her hair over her shoulder; and turned the corner of his music sheet.

'Where's the ring? I need Eula's ring?' That got his attention. Since their kiss, peck, whenever she saw him, a thousand questions burned from his eyes.

'High five? I've found Eula.' She held up her hand, the slap never came. 'Hector's given me time off to take the train to London. I'll give her your ring, you can pass over, and I'll be back in time to cook dinner.'

'Cool.'

So, what's with the sad face? 'You can pass over. No more wandering.'

'Cool.'

Seriously weird. She'd expected a little more enthusiasm, maybe another grateful kiss.

Why had he kissed her? The question swirled around the paper cup. The train pulled into Kings Cross Station, no time to read tea leaves.

Pom took a deep breath and planted her feet on Eula's doorstep. No big deal, routine, a simple deliver and pass over. Eula opened the door, gorgeous . . . still.

Over coffee and chocolate digestives, Pom explained. Shocked by her story, Eula's trembling hand clutched the top of her walking stick. She managed two words.

'Bull crap.'

Eula harboured no regrets. Sure, she'd been sad when

she heard of Apollo's death; but she'd sent him a Dear John letter, long before his leave. Never received. The work of fickle fate. Happily married for fifty-five years; she didn't need or want Apollo's ring. She thanked Pom for coming, and that was that. Apollo's ring returned, almost, mission accomplished.

With legs of stone and a heart of lead, Pom returned to Livingstone Hall. Fat flakes of snow gathered on the driveway; a candle glimmered in the kitchen window. Time to prepare dinner, chilli pumpkin soup and leftover roast. Fingers crossed, Apollo had gone, no need for painful goodbyes.

He lurked by the fridge, a spoon deep in her favourite homemade jam, mischief plastered across his face. A treacherous tear leaked from her eye, etching unexpected relief into her cheek.

Had he been waiting for her? Forsaking the jam, he stepped forward and pulled her into his arms. He was fond of that, and it always felt great.

'Pom. You're back. Hey, what's this? Don't cry, honey.'

'Oh, don't mind me. I get like this when a restless spirit passes. By the way, why are you still here?' His embrace was strong; she should make more effort to pull away.

His fingers folded over her trembling chin, raising her eyes to meet him.

'I couldn't leave without seeing you. I'll miss you, Pomegranate Green.'

'Oh, sure you will. Well, maybe my strawberry jam? Anyway, I can't hang around. I need to press on; everyone's expecting dinner.'

He held her tight, refused to let her pass. 'Pom, I've decided to stay.'

The air froze as she struggled to free herself. Impossible words may be spoken if she stayed cradled in Apollo's heat.

'Yes, well, That's not possible. Sorry, Apollo.'

His knee eased between her thighs. 'Are you sure? Pomegranate Green, do you want me to leave?'

Don't bat those delicious honey orbs at me, Mister.

'Yes ... no ... but it's what has to happen. It's what I do.'

Her face lay cradled, resting in his hands. 'Then we agree. We can work this out?'

'*This?* There's nothing to work out. I can't.' *He'll leave eventually.*

'Why are you afraid? Haven't you felt anything these past few weeks? I thought Eula was it for me, then that day at Cu Chi, I saw you, and I remembered what it was like to be alive. Mad, right?'

'Yes ... no, but it can't go anywhere. I'm a P.I. I swore an oath. It states, 'do not fraternise with your . . . the spirit'. Terrible conflict of interest.'

'To hell with that. No damn red-tape P.I.-bureaucracy is going to keep me from you, from finding out if there is more than just this spark between us.'

'No. Stop. Before I get lost in your magic . . . madness. I'm going to let Hector know I'm back, and you . . . well, you're staying right here.' She took Eula's ring from her pocket, pressed it into his hand and fled.

'Pom. Hell woman, come back here.' His voice echoed through every crevice in the Hall.

Livingstone's spirits held their heads in their hands and groaned.

Built on a foundation of whisper and rumour, Livingstone Hall proved a tough place to leave. Without Apollo, it held no welcome. Time to pack.

A familiar shadow fell across the bedroom mirror.

'Don't fret, hon, I'm here.'

'How the *halibut* . . . Apollo is that you?'

'How many gentlemen are you expecting in your room at this hour?' Pom giggled, *oath, schmoath,* it didn't matter how, only that he was here. She scrambled across the bed, willing him to appear.

'Right here, sugar.' On his knees, in front of her, delicious thoughts simmered behind his amber eyes. 'Told you, I'm not leaving. Not without you.'

Sugar plum fairies! Stop smiling. Pom's fingers itched to touch him, anywhere, everywhere.

'Sweetheart, I'll follow you into hell if need be. Okay?'

'Yes. Big yes.' Her arms flew around his neck, let this one be for me, only me.

Apollo's hand reached around her hip, and settled there; he vowed to stay beside her for eternity, working on their spark. *Eternity*? Pom rolled her eyes. Goddess willing, it wouldn't be that long between kisses.

MORE THAN LIFE ITSELF : CAROL CHALLIS

*I*n the dead of night, footsteps echoed down the main hallway of Livingstone Hall fading into the distance. Ivy Lamington awoke from a restless slumber, instantly alert and angry. A woman's shoe or boot, she thought. Light but determined.

Her instructions had been explicit. 'I want to be alone.'

How dare someone wander around the building when the hotel manager had promised total seclusion. Reluctantly promised. She'd paid for the privilege.

Whoever it was, she'd put them in their place.

She peered into the shadows of her richly appointed room which had seemed so innocuous during the day. A lingering chill seeped from the floorboards and floated around her bare legs as she swung them out of her bed. She ignored the tinge of unease and threw on her favourite floral robe and slippers, determined to confront the intruder.

Out in the hallway, she glanced up and down. Which direction did those footsteps go?

Faint piano notes drifted up the staircase at the end of the hall. It resembled some old-fashioned tune. Soft and lilting.

Shivers jolted down her spine.

Someone was tinkering on that old piano in the corner of the grand ballroom. Tinkering with some proficiency. How dare they! She stiffened her back and marched down the hall.

As a world-class performer herself, she always admired those who practiced their arts but a stranger wandering around playing music in the middle of the night inside a heritage listed mansion that she'd hired for absolute privacy was not admirable and they were soon going to have a piece of her erudite and articulate mind.

The piano's last chord of #A minor resonated in the air. She hesitated at the top of the staircase.

Hairs prickled on the back of her neck. Moonlight slid down the walls illuminating the condescending glares of the old pompous portraits peering from their elevated perches. Just old paintings.

She crept down each step, holding the railing, the third last step creaking into the darkness.

At the base of the staircase, she stopped again, a cold sweat stealing down her spine. Could the unknown musician be a burglar or someone who knew of her operatic fame and was planning to kidnap her for ransom?

But why would they play the piano? Ivy clenched her teeth. After sold-out performances across the continent, she needed this time to herself. Lettice, the hotel manager, had to leave for a weekend conference. The staff had been given time off. Even the hotel chef, who'd premade her gourmet meals, had taken a trip somewhere. It'd be a pity to have them all fired for this discrepancy. The meals had been divine.

The music began again.

Ivy tiptoed towards the grand ballroom now wishing she'd brought a torch. The grey-blue glow of soft moonlight revealed more shadow than light.

She steeled her nerves.

Whoever was playing, she'd catch them red-handed.

Whoever was playing, she'd pierce their soul with her glass-shattering soprano voice.

She spied a large silver candlestick on a side table. If her high notes didn't work, she'd give them a hefty whack on the head.

Ivy placed her hand on the ornate doorknob of the ballroom door. With a deep breath, she wrenched it open.

In a tiny caravan, concealed in the woods, Montgomery Bloom, or Monty as his ghost-buster crew usually called him, tore off his headphones and swore, a piercing scream reverberating in his ear drums.

'What the . . .'

It had been a good night. The ghost detecting equipment he'd set up earlier when he posed as a council inspector was going off the wall. This was the kind of data he needed to get to the truth of so many alleged hauntings.

But who on earth was this strangely familiar woman? She looked more real than ghost. And that scream! The sound spectrum needle had gone over the top and his ears were still ringing.

Monty shook his head, berating himself for nodding off and missing the action.

He needed to replay that scene in the ballroom - this time without the headphones. Monty pressed rewind and viewed the monitor, focusing on the piano in the corner of the screen. Timing was everything in this game. According to his sources, the eerie music playing on a full moon was usually a precursor for paranormal activity.

He pressed play.

Everything was as he'd left it. The screen flickered. Monty blinked. Was that a white wisp materialising at the keyboard?

Rewind. Play. Zoom

OMG!

A white shape, transparent and humanoid. A female in a white dress?

Pause.

Monty's heart-rate doubled, his breath came in gasps.

Play.

Monty listened, cautious of getting another earful of that high pitched soprano scream.

The piano music came through. Light, dainty. The EMF glowed to its full capacity and the temperature gauge dropped.

This haunting looked real. His pulse quickened. His eyes transfixed to the scene.

Another movement caught Monty's eye. A second figure in a floral robe stood close to the camera holding a candlestick above her head. She turned slightly, her eyes wide, her hair wild and untamed and her mouth opening to form a perfect 'O'. Monty wrenched his headphones off.

The readings on the EMF hit the high red mark.

He'd warned hotel management about the legend. The tragic ending. The White Lady's dangerous omen, but the woman had just laughed, telling him that the building had been thoroughly investigated and there was no truth to the ghost stories. The accidents were just that, accidents.

He had to act. He knew the White Lady's need for ruthless justice. He knew he had to act or else the entrancing young lady in the floral gown would be in danger.

Her life depended on him.

No such thing as ghosts. No such thing as ghosts. Ivy repeated the mantra, her eyes riveted to the ghostly woman who seemed to be dissipating into a white mist. The only answer for the transparent pianist was not one she wished to contemplate.

Ghosts can't harm the living. Ghosts can't harm the living. Her heartbeat pounded but her fascination became almost trance-like. *There must be a logical answer.*

She reached the now empty space at the piano and lifted the lid, the moonlight catching the layers of dust beneath the keys. Ivy shivered. The frigid air wrapped around her. Frigid, yet perfumed.

She looked at where the strange apparition had sat. Droplets of water covered the piano seat. Ivy blinked and looked at the ceiling. Was there a leak in this old mansion? Her breath came in shallow bursts. Nothing made sense.

She saw it then. A yellowed piece of music perched on the instrument.

It fluttered as she reached for it.

'The Gypsy Girl's Dream,' she whispered, her eyes following the faded ink of the handwritten notes. The music matched the haunting tune she'd heard earlier. Ivy turned the page over and saw five ominous words.

Meet me in the tower.

Opening the caravan door, Monty cast a final glance at the screen. The motion-activated camera in the tower room flicked on, filling the space with grey light.

If the White Lady followed her usual pattern, she'd move to the tower. That meant he had to get there as well.

Monty plunged into the moonlit forest. That woman's face, beautiful despite the terrified expression, came to him as he ran, dodging fallen branches and bushes. What was she doing in the mansion on her own? The place should be humming with staff. And why did she look so familiar?

The White Lady hauntings, real or not, had led to a series of unfortunate accidents. Misadventures or something a little more sinister?

A cloud covered the moon, plunging the path into darkness.

Monty stopped, gasping in air. He wasn't far now. If he could just get to the tower in time.

The arched doorway beckoned, leading Ivy to the curved stone staircase within. The enclosed air reeked with a cloying scent. Lilac, hyacinth? As if drawn by an invisible force, Ivy climbed the stairs. A small door opened into the brisk night air and the moonlight illuminated the tower, highlighting the stone parapet like a spotlight on a stage. The same white mist that had been at the piano, curled around the ancient stones, and Ivy drew in a breath, mesmerised as each second brought the apparition into sharper detail.

Her long white hair, her slender fingers dripping water, her dark eyes upon her and her mouth forming an unfathomable expression.

The moon slid from the cloud and Monty looked over to the mansion beyond the border fence. There was movement up on the tower. He swore under his breath as he lumbered closer. No doubt another accident would be reported, but this time his devices could prove what was going on. The secrecy would end and the truth would be revealed. But that woman with the gorgeous face and powerful voice would become a statistic if he didn't get there in time.

At the side gate his fingers stumbled over the access code in haste. Full moon, white lady, tragedy. The pattern always played the same way over the years. The jilted White Lady who waited for her long-lost lover in the tower. Her lover who never arrived.

Ivy's senses began to return and along with them; her indignation. This was not real. She'd been tricked into leaving her room and following ghostly sounds, music and perfume in the middle of the night. This staged ghost nonsense might entertain the everyday guest, but this whole escapade wasted a perfectly good night's sleep. She would be telephoning management in the morning to voice her displeasure in no uncertain terms.

She glared at the strange mist-like creature dripping water onto the flagstones. It had to be some kind of projection. She took her eyes from the nebulous form and searched the area for a source. There it was. Some sort of camera with flashing red lights affixed to the door she'd come through. Tricks, smoke and mirrors. She'd seen it all before in the theatre.

'Now look here . . .' Ivy turned back to confront the so-called apparition but the white mist vanished.

'What!' she gasped. An ice-cold grip wrapped around her forearm. She looked down at the transparent spindly fingers clutching her arm and opened her mouth to scream but no sound came out.

Fear stole her breath. Dread filled her lungs.

Monty reached the arched doorway leading to the tower's staircase. Would he be too late?

He took the steps two at a time, his breath rasping from exertion and trepidation.

Sickly perfume churned his stomach. A perfume tinged with stench and damp.

At the tower door, he expected it to be locked or jammed. It stood ajar.

'Is anyone there?' His question went unanswered so he reached for the latch.

Standing in the middle of the tower, he could see the attractive woman in the floral robe, her delicate features creased in bewilderment. She noticed him too; their eyes locking together for a split second. Those eyes, so round, so lustrous . . . and lost.

The door slammed shut.

'Is anyone there?' A male voice, his timbre pleasing despite being out of breath.

Thank goodness. Someone to sort all this nonsense out, Ivy thought. Her knight in shining armour.

Through the partly open door she caught a glimpse of a tall, lanky man with dishevelled hair desperately reaching for the door handle.

The door slammed shut.

The fingers gripping her arm tightened and now she could see the full and terrifying apparition, her facial features contorted in anguish or . . . anger. There was strength in the grip and it was pulling her towards the parapet edge.

Ivy squeezed her eyes shut. This whole experience had gone a too far now.

One hand still gripped the booklet of piano music,

anchoring her to the real world. The sheets opened to *The Gypsy Girl's Dream* from *Bohemian Girl*. That faint piano music she'd heard before was the main aria from that opera. She'd sung it before, a long time ago. She might be trapped in a tower with a deranged white mist but she had the power of logic and her voice. It had to be worth a try. With a shuddering breath, she began to sing.

'*I dreamt that I dwelt in marble halls . . .*'

It was a cursed song. One that was never sung in dressing rooms for fear of jinxing a performance. A song of longing for a lover lost. Ivy kept her eyes on the white lady. The ethereal form wavered slightly, listening. Ivy continued the song's haunting verse.

> '*I had riches too great to count,*
> *could boast of a high ancestral name;*
> *but I also dreamt,*
> *which pleased me most,*
> *that you lov'd me still the same . . .*'

That voice.

Monty yanked on the door handle, the magical sounds floating around him.

He knew that voice.

The lovely Ivy Lamington, the girl who broke his heart in the final year of music college. Ivy, the beautiful soprano, who had sung Arline to his Thaddeus in the stage production of *Bohemian Girl*. The woman whose rise to fame sky rocketed her into the limelight and away from his world.

He pulled harder on the door, her voice surrounding him in melancholy.

The door refused to budge.

What was there to lose? He began to sing, *'That you lov'd me still the same...'*

His voice entwined with the ribbon of sound from Ivy, harmonising together. He heard her falter, then her voice renewed its melody, wrapping breathy tendrils around him. Was it possible? Did she recognise his voice?

The door swung open without warning and there stood Ivy, standing strong against the swirling mist of the White Lady. Her gorgeous eyes held his own, full of fear and yet yearning. Ivy's singing created a layer of protection from the white mist that reached for her. He kept his own voice strong, breathing deeply to project a sound that masked his fear.

Another chorus and the song would end.

One step towards her. Another.

An icy chill pressed into him.

Keep singing.

Closer.

Almost close enough to touch.

The grip from the white mist pulled Ivy almost to the edge of the parapet. *Do not look down.* Her singing had stirred up this strange apparition and she nearly stopped until she heard another voice; deeper tenor joining and harmonising with her tune. She closed her eyes, focusing on the glorious sounds, weaving together, joining as one.

When she opened her eyes, there he was. Tall and serious, singing his soul into her heart.

Around and between, the white mist buffeted them, her icy touch unable to penetrate a cocoon of protection the singing produced. *Keep going*, Ivy urged the man in her mind.

That man, that familiar man with the tousled hair reached for her. A lifeline across time, his arm stretched toward her.

The chorus would end in seconds.

With all her strength, she reached for him. Their fingers almost touching. A sudden flash illuminated the tower. Simultaneously, her hands interlocked with his, warm and secure.

His whole focus was her. His singing was just for her.

'That you lov'd me still the same . . .'

Ivy swallowed. Her voice dropped to a whisper, mouthing the words, realising with true certainty she'd found her bearings at last. She'd finally found him again, her first glorious love. On tiptoes, holding both his hands, she pressed a soft kiss to his lips. A kiss that ended the song. A kiss that started slowly, that warmed gently, that lingered with longing. In that moment the turbulence subsided, the cold fingers on her arm released its grip.

Ivy pulled away to look into her lost lover's eyes. Monty. Dear Monty, whom she'd left behind. The boy she'd never quite forgotten all those years ago. Now he stood there, like he'd always been there. Steadfast and true.

Beyond, she saw a pool of water sparkle in the moonlight, shimmering into darkness. Faint wisps of light lifted, circled briefly around them then scattered into the clear night air. Dissipating into nothing.

'She's gone for now,' whispered Monty.

Ivy nodded. Her heart still pounded.

Monty's familiar smile warmed her, his steady gaze soothed her, his embrace emboldened her. Grasping his hands, Ivy leant back on the old stone parapet.

'And do you love me still?'

'More than life itself.'

~

DUN LÁIDIR : DENISE OGILVIE

The Belgae rose at dawn, painted their powerful bodies, hoisted shields and raised newly sharpened war axes. Their war cry reverberated through the camp, across the valley into the hearts of their enemies.

The battle would free them from the yoke of Roman rule, or send them to join their ancestors, feasting in the otherworld. A man did not give up. To die fighting against Roman oppression was an honour beyond treasure.

Ravens soared above the madness of the battlefield, carrying messages of protection to the Gods. On this day, the Gods of the Otherworld opened their arms in welcome to the bravest of the brave.

Dusk fell on bloodied, broken Belgae warriors as they lay scattered beneath the stone walls of the fort. The stench of blood and decaying flesh filled Chulhain's nostrils. He heard the heavy tread of Roman sandals, knew they were searching for the injured, any man with a sign of life. The footsteps drew closer. Chulhain knew his end was near. As the sword ripped through his body he prayed for a quick death, for the Gods to carry his spirit to Dun Láidir, resting place of his ancestors, buried deep below the Roman fort.

He closed his eyes. His woman knelt at his side, her red hair merging into the splay of blood as he drifted into the darkness.

'Róisín,' he called.

'I will come for you,' she whispered, as the shadows of the fallen surrounded them. 'It is foreseen by the ancients.'

Ruby McGrath sighed. The motorway around Basingstoke had been a nightmare. Google maps indicated that it was just over two hours from London to Livingstone Hall. Laughing at the thought, she glanced at the dashboard clock and cursed. Seven-thirty already. Over an hour late for the retreat.

Spectral birch trees flung shadowy silhouettes across the rutted lane. At the next bend the Gothic façade of Livingstone Hall emerged from the woodland, its sandstone walls glowing red and yellow in the setting sun. The Hall was breathtaking in the half-dark of the autumn twilight. Flashes of unexpected lightning made the hairs on her arms rise.

The photo on the brochure had not prepared her for the magnificent sight of Livingstone Hall. In the half-dark, it had the gravitas of a medieval castle.

The tyres crunched on the white gravel driveway as she pulled in next to a row of cars. Tucking strands of auburn hair behind her ears, she hurried from her car, knowing she was last to arrive. The others would already be at dinner. She knew she should have rung to let them know she would be late.

Ruby pushed open the heavy oak doors and gasped. A grand staircase, at the centre of the entrance hall, curved up to the first floor. To the left, ancient crossed swords hung from the wall above the reception desk. On the opposite wall, suits of armour stood on either side of an open fire. Despite the warmth, a chill ran through her body. She walked over to the desk, her heels clicking on the marble floor, and pressed the brass bell on the counter. To her surprise a door in the oak panelled wall slid open and an elderly man stepped out. He wore an old-fashioned tweed suit with brass buttons. A black silk cravat complemented his crisp white shirt. His silver hair was cropped short above the stiff collar of his shirt.

'Welcome.' His voice was soft. Ruby strained to hear him.

'Hi,' she said. 'I'm Ruby McGrath. I have a booking.'

She leaned on the counter and watched him open a large ledger. He ran a bony finger down the columns.

'Ah, there you are miss,' he whispered. 'You're in the Lucius Gallus room.'

He lifted a heavy, antiquated iron key from a drawer beneath the desk.

'Up the stairs and to the left,' he said as he handed it over. 'The room names are on the doors.'

Ruby climbed the stairs and found her room. No time to admire all the red velvet, she dropped her bag on the four-poster bed and then left, locking the door behind her. Downstairs, a tall, blonde woman, in a severe black suit now waited at the reception desk where the old man had just been.

Her lapel badge identified her as Lettice Chapman, Manager, Livingstone Hall. Her crisp voice cut through the air. 'Can I help you?'

'Um, yes,' Ruby stammered. 'I didn't get a chance to ask the old man where to go for dinner?'

'Old man?' The woman's sharp features softened. 'Oh, you mean Hector. What did he do?'

'He signed me in and gave me a key.' She pulled the key from her shoulder bag.

'The Gallus Room. He would, wouldn't he?'

Ruby had no idea what she was talking about. Her stomach grumbled.

With a raised brow, Lettice pointed to double doors near the side of the fireplace. The style was pure ancient castle rather than restored manor house. 'You'll find your group in there.'

Ruby opened the dining room door. Seven people sat around a large, round table. A dark-haired man stood up and smiled at her.

'You must be Ruby,' he said. 'Glad you made it.'

'The traffic. . .' she started to say.

'I know,' he said. 'It can be a real bother on a Friday afternoon. Still, you're here and that's all that matters.'

He pulled out a chair. 'My name's Cullen,' he said.

The other six introduced themselves.

Cullen said, 'Do you want to tell us something about yourself?'

Ruby trembled. She hated speaking in front of others. She took a deep breath and tried not to mumble, sure that the group would snigger at her answer. 'I write fiction, well, romantic historical fiction.'

'Then you've come to just the right place,' Cullen said. 'The history of Livingstone Hall is amazing. Did you know that somewhere beneath the cellar are the remains of a Roman temple?'

'I did read something about that,' Ruby replied.

'What room are you staying in?' a woman asked.

'The Lucius Gallus room, whoever that is.'

'Only the first Roman commander of the fort this place is built on,' someone else said.

While they ate dinner, drank wine and talked history, Ruby did her best to remember everyone's names.

After dessert, Cullen stood up and stretched. 'I'm off to catch up on reading. We've got a lot to get through tomorrow morning.'

The group disbanded and Ruby climbed the stairs. Her

head spun from the extra glass of wine. Portraits of ancient lords stared down at her from the walls. At the top of the stairs a marble bust sat on a blackwood table. The brass label identified him as Lucius Gallus. Her room was next to the bust, as if this Lucius guarded her door.

Ruby twisted the key in the lock and opened the door. The warmth of the central heating flowed over her. A huge four-poster bed took up most of the floor space and a door lead into a small but modern bathroom. The bed was high, with a step stool at its side. Crimson velvet curtains, matching the bed drapes, covered a corner window. Opening the curtains, ribbons of bright moonlight streamed through the latticed window. Outside, the swaying shadows of deep-rooted oak trees resembled sinister combatants circling each other across a battlefield. Something caught her eye and she shuddered. A raven flapped its wings and flew from the parapet beneath her window. Ruby shivered despite the warmth of the room and pulled the curtains closed.

She picked up a brochure from the bedside table and sank into the comfy old armchair next to the window. The history of Livingstone Hall intrigued her. According to the brochure there had been a settlement on this site since Roman times. The current hall went back to the seventeenth century. It had remained in the hands of the same family for over four hundred years until recently. There were whispers that a famous rock star now owned the house after the family had fallen onto hard times.

Ruby stood up and stretched. She changed into her pyjamas and climbed up into the bed. The soft mattress wrapped around her body. She picked up her book and snuggled into the warm folds of the duvet.

Sometime during the night Ruby woke. The book lay open at her side. She glanced at the bedside clock. It was 2.22 am and the room was cold. She pulled the cover up over her chin.

Something rattled in the bathroom. Her body trembled despite the warmth of the bed.

The sound grew louder. She must have left the window open. She climbed out of bed. Her feet sank into the thick carpet. Then Ruby cursed as her foot hit the bedside table. Despite the throbbing pain in her big toe, she hobbled to the bathroom. The curtain fluttered in the shadows. A man stood below the window. Moonlight shone like a halo around his body. Ruby froze. She opened her mouth to scream. Her throat tightened. The scream never eventuated.

Dark hooded eyes clouded the man's haunted gaze. Two long, black plaits hung down each side of his handsome, but melancholy face. His arms were bare. Silver armbands encased rippling muscles. He whispered one word, 'Róisín', as he stepped back into the shadows and disappeared. The curtain fluttered in the chill breeze. Ruby rubbed her eyes and wondered if she was dreaming. She closed the window and crawled back in the warmth of the bed where she drifted into a restless sleep.

Ruby gripped the bannister as she came down the stairs. Her head swirled with thoughts of last night, and her dreams of the handsome stranger.

Lettice looked up from the reception desk.

'You look a little pale,' she said. 'Was everything satisfactory with your room?'

Should she say anything? Who would believe her anyway? An Iron-Age warrior haunting her dreams. She shook her head in reply. 'No, everything was fine. The bed was comfortable, despite the climb.'

Lettice laughed. 'Most of our guests say the same thing.'

The tantalising smell of an English breakfast wafted from

the dining room. Ruby joined her group at the table. Rory – oh good, she remembered his name – jumped up and pulled out a chair for her. She thanked him with a smile. Moments later a young waitress appeared at Ruby's shoulder and set down a plate filled with bacon, eggs, hash browns and sausages.

'Thank you,' she said, patting her stomach. 'I didn't realise how hungry I was until I saw this.'

Cullen cleared his throat. 'I'm sure you've read the agenda for today, but just as a quick reminder, we'll spend the morning in here at the workshop. After lunch, you're free to keep writing or wander around the grounds. Lots of inspiration out there. Looks like it's going to be sunny.'

The day flew by in a flurry of activity. After lunch, the group went their separate ways. Ruby spent the afternoon in her room working on her latest novel. From the desk, she looked out over the manicured lawns and gardens, imagining the grounds alive with Roman soldiers. Men practicing their sword skills and drilling in the forecourt; the day to day work of an operational Roman fort. A bell rang in the distance, breaking her thoughts. She looked at her watch, amazed that it was already time for dinner.

After a sumptuous dinner, the group assembled in the library. Ruby gazed around the room. Hundreds of books filled the timber shelves lining the walls. A fire roared in the hearth.

'Wine?' Cullen appeared in the doorway with a bottle in one hand and a glass in the other.

Ruby nodded and accepted the drink as she sank into the well-worn chesterfield sofa.

Ten minutes later Lettice appeared.

'I thought some of you might be interested in a tour of the house?' she said.

'Only if it includes the Roman ruins in the basement,' Cullen said. 'I've heard so much about them and Ruby was just telling me how much she loved the Roman history of Gloucestershire.'

The rest of the group made comments such as 'join you on the next one,' as they absorbed the cosy warmth of the fire along with their ports and whiskies.

Lettice said. 'Be warned it gets cold in the basement. I'd suggest wearing a jacket.'

Five minutes later Ruby and Cullen joined Lettice in the reception area. Ruby had grabbed her woollen shawl. She wrapped it around her shoulders, and with Cullen at her side, followed Lettice down a narrow passageway to a door. Lettice switched on a torch. The beam lit up rough stone walls. As soon as Ruby stepped in she felt a chill and wrapped the shawl tighter around her body. She followed Lettice down a tight spiralling stone staircase. The further they went, the colder the air became and she shivered.

'Are you alright?' Cullen whispered from behind.

'Just a bit cold,' Ruby replied. 'I wonder how much further we have to go.'

'Just about there,' Lettice said as she turned a corner and stepped down onto a rough, cobbled surface.

A tall stone stood in the centre of the room. Ruby inhaled. The cold air hit her lungs and the room spun. When her head cleared, she found herself alone. The air carried a tang of damp, like a forest floor after heavy rain.

The next second, Ruby blinked hard as she found herself standing next to a stream. Slivers of daylight, filtering through thick, overhanging oak branches touched the standing stone. Carved into the stone was the image of a man killing a bull. Torchbearers stood either side of him. From her studies, she knew this was an altar to the Roman god Mithras. She heard a rustle in the shadows. A man stepped forward. The man was the dark-haired warrior from her dream. Once again, he held out his hand to her and she reached out to him. His skin was rough against hers. He was a flesh and blood man. She looked into his eyes and felt safe, as if she already knew him.

'Róisín,' he said. 'You have come to me at last.' His deep, velvety voice reverberated through the forest.

Ruby parroted him, 'Ro-sheen?'

'It is me, Chulhain,' he whispered as he caressed her hand. 'You have returned to Dun Láidir. Now, at last, I can rest with my ancestors.'

'I'm not Rosheen, I'm Ruby,' she said. 'Who are you?'

His calloused hand was warm to her touch. He spoke of a great battle against the Romans. His people slaughtered, their bodies thrown into a mass grave at the order of their commander, Lucius Gallus.

He told of the Roman fort built over Dún Láidir, the ancestral burial mound of his people. His soul and those of his people were searching for their resting place, to join their ancestors.

'Why me?' Ruby asked.

'My people, the Belgae, know you have been sent to return us to our ancestors. The druids foresaw the battle. They told of a woman, descended from our bloodline, who would one day return. We have been waiting a long time. You are that woman. The time has come.'

As he spoke a mist descended over them. Ruby lost sight of Culhain. His hands released hers. She cried out to him but the forest fell silent. She closed her eyes and a tear rolled down her cheek. The air chilled again. Ruby opened her eyes. The mist had disappeared and she was back in the basement.

Cullen stood next to her, his arms wrapped around her trembling body.

'Are you alright?' he said. 'I thought you were going to faint.'

'I'm fine,' Ruby said. 'I don't really like enclosed spaces. Can we go back upstairs?'

'Of course,' Lettice said. 'I think you've seen enough.'

'What do you know about a place called Dún Láidir?' Ruby asked Lettice.

'I haven't heard that name for a long time,' Lettice replied. 'There is an old folk tale that says we are standing on an ancient burial mound, but short of pulling down Livingstone Hall I guess we'll never know.'

'Have you thought of changing the name of my room?' Ruby said to Lettice.

'Yes,' she replied. 'We've just been waiting for the right time.'

Ruby smiled knowingly as she turned and climbed the stairs.

∾

FOREVER MINE : LOUISE REYNOLDS

a crack of lightning rent the heavens as Clare Cardew pulled her car to a stop in the forecourt of Livingstone Hall Country House Hotel and Spa. Against a sullen grey sky, the split-second electrostatic charge illuminated a honeyed stone façade, with flat gables peaked as a witch's hat and black-eyed mullioned windows.

Clare dropped her head forward, rested it between her hands on the steering wheel and closed her eyes. This was like a Hallowe'en scene from a Hollywood movie.

There was no help for it but to switch off the engine and push the car door open. It promptly blew shut. 'And so it starts,' she muttered. Only her therapist's words forced her out of the car and into the freezing cold November morning. Ghosts can't hurt you. They're not real.

But Dr May wasn't spending All Hallows Eve in the most haunted house in England. When dead souls roamed, even Clare's sanguine doctor might change her mind.

Inside the foyer, Clare unwound her scarf, her gaze tracking around the vast entry. It had all the accoutrements of a Jacobean house: armaments on the walls, heavily polished oak furniture, and an abundance of pewter and classic blue and white Delft pottery. But the gossamer web of phosphorescent light shimmering against the crimson flock wallpaper on the stairs rather spoiled the effect. A 'White Lady' ghost Clare supposed, squaring her shoulders. Boringly *de rigueur* for every ancient house.

A wave of cold air blasted her, freezing her flippant thought.

Grey Lady if you please.

A touchy ghost. Making light of her fears was part of Dr May's latest advice. She'd been treating Clare with immersion therapy, but after watching what seemed to be the entire Hollywood canon of ghost and horror movies, Clare still wasn't cured. Humour was the latest ploy.

A door slammed and a woman emerged from a room down the hall and moved forward with a smile. 'Miss Cardew?'

'Clare, please.' Clare put down her overnight bag and held out her hand.

'And I'm Diana Bracechurch, the winter manager. Welcome to Livingstone Hall. We're so thrilled that Cardew's is reviewing us again. It's been some years since we last appeared in your guide and things have a way of changing, haven't they?'

Carefully maintained control was evident in the ash blonde, immaculately arranged hair and the rigorously upright posture and yet there was something else, an edgy alertness that made Clare's skin tingle.

'They do,' Clare agreed. 'I'm delighted to be here. It's such a beautiful house.'

'I'll show you to your room.' Diana gestured towards the stairs and fell into an obviously rehearsed routine. 'The house is terribly old. Apparently, there was a pagan place of worship here before the abbey was built. That managed to survive the Dissolution but burned down in 1604. This part of the house is Jacobean.'

And Georgian to the rear Clare had noted earlier with professional interest, a mix of styles that sat uneasily together. More than that, it vibrated with the presence of at least a dozen restless souls, the psychic energy ratcheted to a tense, whistling high. She gritted her teeth and tried to block it.

They reached the bottom of the staircase and Clare took a deep breath. The shimmer was still there, waiting. 'Haunted I take it. How lovely.' She rubbed her hands together with the sort of enthusiastic glee that readers of *Cardew's Great Britain Hotel Guide* might exhibit. Especially Americans who were mad for ghosts. 'I can't wait.'

Liar. The accusation blew into her ear accompanied by a current of Harris tweed and Old Port pipe tobacco.

Diana turned and fixed her with a steely look. 'It *was* haunted but the new owners had the place gone over when they took it on. They had an Anglican vicar, a Catholic priest and a rabbi in, three for the price of one you might say.' She chuckled at her own joke, her hand resting on the balustrade. 'They wanted all that ghost nonsense gone. People might say it's good for business but I'm not so sure.' A muscle in her neck twitched.

The phosphorescent light wavered as Clare followed Diana up the staircase. She gave it a small wave and the warmth of the hall dropped for a moment.

'And we had a Wiccan for good measure,' the manager continued before brightening. 'Anyway, the place is clean as a whistle these days.'

The woman was either a fool or a liar. The house was teeming with ghosts.

At the top of the stairs they turned right, and passed through a glorious gallery panelled in oak and lined with portraits before turning down a narrower corridor with gently sloping floors.

'Here's your room, dear.' Diana opened the door and stood

back allowing Clare to enter. Soft lighting and a small fire warmed the room, which was charmingly decorated with Liberty floral print draperies and scattered with pretty Georgian furniture.

'It's charming.' As she moved towards the fire the tinkle of childish laughter sounded from the adjoining bathroom. Clare froze, her hands outstretched to the fire, and turned towards Diana. The woman clutched at the pearls circling her throat, her face drained of colour but meeting Clare's gaze she shook herself. 'A little problem with the drains no doubt. You know how old houses are.'

Diana took her leave and dense silence fell, broken only by the snap of flames. Clare's pulse hammered hard. 'I know you're here but you won't get any joy from me,' she said.

There was no answer so Clare pulled out her laptop, crossed to the small desk and opened it. The screen flickered and went dark.

'Very funny.'

When the screen obligingly sprung to life she muttered, 'Thank you.' It never hurt to be polite to ghosts.

After she'd settled in and made a few preparatory notes, Clare set off to explore the house. She started in the long gallery where a fitful sun threw slabs of muted light through the mullioned windows. Large rugs, soft underfoot, muffled her footsteps as she walked, stopping here and there to examine a painting or object in a display case. It was as she stepped back from a painting, tilting her head to the side to better view it, that she walked straight into a solid body.

She shrieked and, heart pounding, turned. The man standing before her was most definitely flesh and blood, with eyes the colour of green slate and hair like a peaty stream tumbling over rocks. He reached out to steady her. 'I'm sorry, I didn't mean to frighten you.'

She took another step back, her hand resting at her throat as she willed her racing pulse to slow. She'd thought the gallery had been empty but this man seemed to have appeared from thin air. 'Where did you come from?'

He pointed to a small corridor at the other end of the gallery. 'I'm sorry but these rugs muffle everything. I saw you there and wasn't sure whether to disturb you or not. Anyway, I'm Marc Richards.' He held out a hand and Clare took it, reassured by the firm grip.

'Clare. Clare Cardew.'

'Are you alright?'

She gave a shaky laugh. 'Yes, I think so. It's just . . .' she withdrew her hand and crossed her arms around her body, repressing a shiver. 'It's this house. It's lovely but . . .'

His eyes softened. 'I totally understand. Listen, unless someone else turns up I believe we're the only guests, so would you care to join me for dinner later?'

It would be good to have a dinner companion, and such an attractive one at that. But there was a fragile sadness about him that made her hesitate.

'It might be a bit too formal sitting at our own individual tables in a big empty room,' he added.

It really would be silly to sit alone at separate tables. Clare smiled. 'That would be lovely.'

Marc was waiting when she entered the dining room. A table in the bay of a long window had been laid for two, with crisp white napery, polished silver and sparkling glassware. With the drapes drawn against the black night and the warm candlelight, it was an oasis in the otherwise empty room.

Was it Marc's warm eyes on her or something else that had her nerves skittering as she approached the table? He stood up, a small frown pleating his forehead. 'You look worried. If you've changed your mind...'

'No, it's this house. You know they call it the most haunted house in England.' She took the seat he held out for her.

'I had heard that.' He took the seat opposite. In the candlelight his eyes warmed to a rich whisky colour.

'And it's Hallowe'en tonight,' she said. 'At least there are no scary decorations. The atmosphere is weird enough without that.' She picked up her napkin and laid it across her lap.

He studied the table for a few moments and when he glanced up his eyes searched hers. 'So you can see them too?'

Clare let out a long breath. 'I don't actually *see* them. I can only see a bit of light here and there, or feel a change in temperature, or an uncomfortable feeling. Sometimes words come into my mind in strange voices, from nowhere.' She took a sip from her water glass. 'You said 'too'.'

'Oh, I see them. They're actually a very good class of ghost here. As you'd expect.' He cast a wry glance around the room. With its vaulted ceiling, ornate plasterwork and silk carpets this was no ordinary house.

A waiter approached and handed them menus. After he'd left, Clare said, 'You seem awfully relaxed about ghosts.'

'I'm used to it. They don't frighten me.' There it was again, that slightly sad smile.

He leaned forward, and gestured her to do the same. He was so close that she thought, just for a moment, he might be about to kiss her. But he lowered his voice to a whisper. 'I'm contracted to P.I.S.'

Surprised by her disappointment at the non-kiss she leaned back and arched a brow in enquiry. He remained where he'd been, leaning across the table, and crooked a finger, drawing her back again.

'Paranormal Investigative Service,' he whispered.

'You're a gho–'

'Shh! Ghosts aren't stupid. Apparently P.I.S. was engaged some time ago to come up here but they arrived in a bloody great van with their name on the side.' He shook his head. 'Amateurs. I'm a freelancer and work in a totally different way.'

'So you don't use electronic devices?' she asked.

'I don't need them. I can see every single ghost in this room.'

Clare's pulse spiked as she forced herself to gaze about the empty dining room. Something had made her skin tingle when she'd entered the room but all she could see were bare tables for two or four with empty chairs drawn up to them.

'You're not afraid, are you?' he asked.

'Of course I am. I've had a paranormal experience in just about every old home I review.'

Recognition lit his face. 'Cardew. Of *Cardew's Guides*?'

She nodded. 'It seems like people can't buy a Grade II listed property without thinking about turning it into a hotel. It's a good day when I get to review a spanking new, up to the minute hotel.'

'Then why not get a different job?'

He made it sound so simple that Clare let out a sigh. 'I'm the last Cardew. My great-great-grandfather started the guide in the Victorian era and there's been a Cardew at the helm ever since. To be honest with you while the name still has some cachet, with all the online review sites these days it's a dying trade.'

'So fold it and do something different. Nothing is worse than being terrified.'

The wine arrived and they waited as it was poured and tasted. When they were alone again, Clare continued. '*Cardew's Guide* was my father's life passion but he's very ill. I can't bear to close it while he's still alive.' The image of her father as she'd said goodbye to him before this round of reviews came back to her. 'So I've committed to keep it going while he's alive and that means doing the rounds of these ghost-infested houses.'

'Perhaps if I describe them to you it would help.' He took a sip of wine. 'Over there, at the corner table, is an American soldier with an assortment of jams.'

'How come you don't drop your voice now?' Clare asked.

'They seem to like it when you're able to see them. Perhaps it's validation that something of them still remains. Or pride in their ability to materialise. They just don't like the idea of 'experts' prodding them so it's not a good idea to mention G-busting.

'Anyway, just by the door is a cheeky little boy running amok through the place.'

'He might be the little boy I heard laughing in my bathroom earlier.'

'And standing guard over by the decanters on the sideboard is a bluff old fellow who seems to be in charge. Totally harmless though.'

The rattle of crystal from the sideboard disagreed.

Clare sat back and smiled. 'You're wonderful. You make them sound like real people. I'm almost starting to relax.'

We know something you don't know. The child's gleeful voice swirled around her. Startled, she glanced at Marc but it seemed he hadn't heard.

He was lost in thought, his finger tracing over the tablecloth. Finally, he glanced up. 'They were real people' he insisted. 'I can't tell you how much that helps.'

'Helps what?'

He shook his head and changed the subject.

As he walked her back through the long gallery after dinner he turned to her, his eyes soft. 'Would it be a bit forward if I asked to kiss you?'

It was a curiously formal but charming request and since Clare had been thinking of kissing him for the last hour, she smiled. As their lips met, warmth flooded her body and sensing her response he changed the angle of the kiss, his arm pulling her closer, his tongue pushing deeper. He tasted of whisky and coffee and urgency.

At last he pulled away but left his hands resting lightly on her arms. He looked directly into her eyes. 'It's going to be alright, Clare.' And with that he walked away.

Later that evening, as she tossed in a tangle of sheets and duvet, her dreams crowded with a hundred strange images, Clare woke to a high, shrill scream and the sound of an ambulance siren.

When she came down to breakfast, only a white-faced Diana stood near the buffet, nervously rearranging silver.

'What happened last night?' Clare began.

The other woman's face shuttered. 'Nothing to concern yourself with. One of the staff had a nasty accident but everything is taken care of now.'

'Has Mr Richards breakfasted yet?'

Diana gave her a sharp look. 'He left early this morning. Now if you'll excuse me.'

Clare was sorry not to see him again. The lingering kiss had replayed in her mind all night. She'd hoped it might be the start of something, but now it was to be nothing more than a pleasant memory.

After breakfast Clare set off to look at the chapel in the woods. Advertised as the perfect place to have a wedding, she couldn't help thinking as she trudged along a sunken path overhung with dripping foliage, that it was anything but. No doubt in summer, there'd be sun and flowers to banish the gloom. As the path broke free from the woods and opened into a clearing, Clare's breath caught. The chapel, starkly white, rose from the midst of a dank graveyard, the bare branches of birch trees created black woven lace in the mist. She suppressed a shiver and walked closer. Five minutes' quick examination would be enough for the guide and then she'd leave Livingstone Hall forever.

Desiccated leaves mounded up against the double doors in the porch. Clare inserted the key Diana had given her and pulled the door open, sweeping the leaves aside. Inside, the chapel was freezing cold but with its breathtakingly beautiful interior no wonder it was so popular for weddings.

It was a few moments before she realised she wasn't alone. A man sat in the back pew and her heart leapt at the sight of the tousled, peat-coloured curls gleaming in the dark.

He hadn't gone after all. Had she told him last night that she'd be here in the morning? Maybe he'd decided to wait here to say goodbye.

'Marc.'

For a moment, she thought he hadn't heard. She moved closer, her footsteps unnaturally loud on the marble floor, just as he rose from the pew. 'I'm sorry, Clare,' he said, his back still turned.

Confused she took another step and was only an arm's length away as he turned.

Expressionless eyes leached of colour in a pallid face stared at her as his hand, with a ghastly deep cut at the wrist, reached towards her. 'Clare. Beloved.'

'No.' She took several steps back, her mind screaming with horror and confusion. 'I don't understand.'

That same sad smile quirked the bloodless lips. 'No doubt

Diana told you there was an accident last night. There was no accident. It was time.'

'No.' The whimper escaped as bile rose in her throat. 'But P.I.S. You told me—'

'That was true. It's how I originally found my spiritual home. All I was waiting for was a partner for the hereafter.' He moved towards her, his face stretched in a ghastly smile.

She backed away and then ran into the central aisle, as a cacophony of voices started; a low, male voice speaking an unintelligible Celtic language, a child almost hysterical with laughter. Others, too many others.

'Stop!' A disembodied woman's voice sounded older than time itself as it echoed through the chapel.

The voices died instantly.

'You cannot do this. She is not a Compton-Barr,' the woman's dreadful voice pronounced.

The Celtic male voice, low with erotic insinuation, answered. 'But she will be his. For eternity.'

Clare launched herself towards the chapel doors just as they slammed shut.

HOW THE HAUNTINGS OF LIVINGSTONE HALL CAME TO LIFE

We are a writing group called 'The Saturday Ladies' Bridge Club'. Why? Because we always meet on Saturdays, we're all female and some of us live *this* side of Melbourne's West Gate Bridge and some of us on *that*, so someone always has to drive across the bridge to get to our meetings.

We live in Melbourne, Australia and 'the bridge' is a big deal here. We're a city divided by a river and . . . a bridge.

So our name is an 'in' joke, but we love it, even if we do have to always explain it.

The idea for a ghost anthology came about during our end-of-year meeting, which was over lunch with lots of wine. Two of us were writing romances that featured ghosts or ghost hunters, and one of us is a ghost tour guide. We sensed something of a theme.

Friendly peer pressure saw us playing around with the idea of short stories, all involving ghosts and all set in a fictional country house in the rolling green hills of England. One glass of wine lead to another and now here we are.

We hope you've enjoyed your break at Livingstone Hall and enjoyed meeting our ghosts. We certainly enjoyed writing their stories for you.

Please rate your stay by leaving a review on your book-buying website of choice.

Be warned: we are already contemplating our next anthology!

ABOUT EBONY MCKENNA

Ebony McKenna is best known as the creator of the four-part young adult ONDINE series, about a teen girl whose pet ferret starts talking with a Scottish accent.

Her other novels include *1916-Ish*, a time slip romantic adventure, and *Robyn and the Hoodettes*, a gender flip adventure on the classic legend.

Her latest novel is *The Girl and The Ghost*, released for Hallowe'en, 2017.

Come and waste some time with her on social media

website ebonymckenna.com
email author@ebonymckenna.com
facebook facebook.com/EbonyMcKenna/
twitter @EbonyMckenna

ABOUT SARAH J WOLFE

Sarah J Wolfe has been telling stories since she was a child, when she entertained her parents on long car trips with the adventures of her teddy bear and the antics of the lions that lived under the bed.

The Hauntings of Livingstone Hall is her publishing debut.

She writes romances with ghosts, though sometimes without ghosts.

Born and brought up in England, Sarah lives in Melbourne, Australia, with her husband, dogs and vegetable patch.

Come and say hello at facebook.com/sarahjwolfeauthor/

ABOUT ALISON STUART

Mystery, history, romance and ghosts . . . Award winning Australian author, Alison Stuart learned her passion for history from her father. She has been writing stories since her teenage years but it was not until 2007 that her first full-length novel was published. Alison has now published eight full-length historical romances and a collection of her short stories.

Her soldier heroes may come from her varied career as a lawyer in the military and fire services. These days when she is not writing she is travelling and routinely drags her long suffering husband around battlefields and castles.

Visit Alison's website at www.alisonstuart.com and sign up to her newsletter for exclusive free reads, contests and more.

She's also on facebook at facebook.com/AlisonStuartWriter/ and twitter as @alisonstuart14

ABOUT ELIZA RENTON

Between the books in the library, Eliza dreamt of being a ballerina at the Royal Ballet or an academic. Neither of which panned out.

Dogs love her, children tolerate her, cats dismiss her. On a good day, she believes in eternal love and soul mates.

"The course of true love never did run smooth."

— WILLIAM SHAKESPEARE

But it's all about the journey, not the destination. Yes?

Published in short story, Eliza is working on her first full-length romance, set in London, England and West Africa.

Happy to hear from you.
elizarenton@gmail.com
facebook.com/ElizaRenton

ABOUT CAROL CHALLIS

Carol Challis delights in scaring people, telling the chilling tales of spirits and hauntings of the historic maritime village where she leads ghost tours at night. It's not unusual for ghosts to weave their way into her written work along with the mystery of the natural world. When she's not scaring people, she is a wife, mother and Jill-of-all-trades and occasionally a nature tour guide. She's a thoroughly all-round greenie with a degree in science communication and a qualification in professional writing and editing.

"The possession of knowledge does not kill the sense of wonder and mystery. There is always more mystery."

— ANAÏS NIN

Come and meet Carol at facebook.com/carol.challis

ABOUT DENISE OGILVIE

Denise Ogilvie's debut novel - writing as Isabel Ogilvie - was *The Luchair Stones*, a children's fantasy adventure published by Phoenix Yard Books in London in 2014.

A former librarian, Denise has spent her lifetime writing short stories and has been shortlisted, commended and longlisted in multiple writing awards.

She'd love to hear from you deniseogilvie@hotmail.com

ABOUT LOUISE REYNOLDS

Louise Reynolds is an author of contemporary romantic fiction published by Penguin Random House.

On receiving her library card at the age of six she borrowed her first book, an illustrated story about onions. Over the years she progressed from vegetables to romance. It was a logical step to take her love of romance novels to the next stage and tell her own stories.

Set in both the city and Australia's outback, her books have been described as warm and witty feel-good reads.

Let's talk! Find out more about me and my books here:
www.louisereynolds.net
louise@louisereynolds.net
facebook: louise.reynolds.798
twitter: @LouiseHReynolds